The Montegard Murder

Paul A. Copenhagen

To my darling wife, who listens patiently to all my ideas.

To my mother and father, who instilled in me a deep love of reading.

To my family, who encouraged me every step along the way.

To my editors, Christopher, Deborah, and Casey.

Thank you

PROLOGUE

The courtroom was almost empty that April morning as the jury deliberated. On one side sat three attorneys representing the families of half a dozen slain soldiers and a dozen more wounded soldiers and officers. Of course, as the plaintiffs, the wounded had been brought in, in their dress uniforms, with their Purple Heart medals each polished to a light shine. There was conveniently enough space on the front bench for six more people, the six fallen who had not been 'lucky' enough to survive their injuries. On the other side Sylvia Montegard, the president and owner of Montegard Arms and Munitions, sat with her team of attorneys. Her dark hair tied up in a power bun, she wore a professional, but not designer made, dress. The entire trial had seen her arrive in her lawyer's car, dressed in off the rack but, mid-priced well fitting clothes, and eating at local establishments including the courthouse's cafeteria. Her jewelry was trimmed back and her makeup was simple. With a net worth of three hundred twenty-two million dollars, the appearance of wealth was carefully removed from the jury's view.

There were three lawyers on the defendant's side: two of Sylvia's own, and one representing the insurance company which provided a twenty million dollar insurance policy. Charlie Callahan sat in the first row behind the defendant's side of the courtroom. Sometimes he hated his job. As an insurance adjuster it was his job to investigate the claims as they came along and pay what the company actually owed. 'Not a penny more, not a penny less' was the saying around the office. Handling hundreds of claims each year, of course there were times when he paid out on claims he didn't want to. Those 'ruinous' injury claims where someone's entire life was turned upside down by a slip and fall in a grocery store or a bumper scrape where the damage is buffed out drove him nuts, but when juries said 'you pay', he paid. On the other side there were times when the victims were real; when the injuries were prevalent and he had to stare at the person face to face, and tell them he would be paying less than what they wanted to get. American Standard Indemnity needed to be profitable, after all, and claims were the expenses of the insurance industry. So when he received direction from on high to save a little money off of the policy limits, he did it, even if he didn't like it.

This was one of those times. With twenty million dollars on the line, his bosses knew that a jury could order a verdict close to the limit, but with the plaintiffs' collective demand at 18 million, one million for each injured man, Charlie and the defense attorneys were confident, and had reassured his bosses that they were fine. Charlie sighed gently as the courtroom waited for the jury to finish their deliberations. The rest of the gallery had been dismissed and now only a few people tied to the trial remained in the courtroom. Charlie sent off a text to his boss informing her that the jury was still in deliberations and he would be here a while longer. He then switched to the text conversation with his wife and asked her what they wanted to do for dinner that night. That's when the bailiff announced the jury would be re-entering. The doors opened to let the gallery back in. People shuffled in. Charlie looked around as he straightened his shirt and tie and sat up straight, watching those who entered. Michael Ambrose, one of the key witnesses for the plaintiffs, took a seat in the second row on that side of the courtroom. More people filled the gallery, mostly reporters and a few people who were just interested in the case. A graying man that Charlie recognized as Colonel David

Elmore sat down on the defendant's side, a few rows back. He had been the point of contact in the investigation into the use of the experimental M87, a new grenade developed for the US Army that had rolled forward into initial field tests and training under Elmore's command. The eighteen casualties and injuries were all his men. Elmore swore up and down that he knew nothing of the defects that led to the M87's faulty use, and had provided ample documentation to show that the grenade had been delivered to his use after thorough testing in the lab and the field by Montegard Arms. Similar paperwork had come to Charlie as a result of his investigation into his insured's activities in creating the M87. From start to finish, the process was deemed by independent experts to be industry standard and above board. Of course there were flaws noted in the initial testing, but they had been fixed after QC's first and second round of checks. The grenade itself did work well and delivered on its promise, but eighteen deaths and serious injuries said that something was wrong. One training accident on a live fire grenade range was to be expected. Two might be considered abnormal or high. But eighteen? The numbers simply pointed to something else: a known and obvious flaw in the design. The plaintiffs called on experts that worked on grenade design and munitions manufacturing to explain potential flaws. The defense countered with their own experts pointing out that the designs had been quality checked on several occasions.

Then the victims had testified. Unlike the M67, which the M87 was designed to replace, the M87 came with a launching sling that, once the grenade was launched from the sling, would remove the pin, hurtling it at a higher accuracy and greater range than the M67 being thrown by hand was normally capable of. The victims testified that they had practiced repeatedly and successfully with the training version of the sling to get the motion right. Training videos were shown. A video of one such incident that left good soldiers crippled and killed was shown to the jury despite motions from the defense to quash them. While not all the videos were shown, the judge agreed that it was likely germane to the case to show at least one video. The victims testified that each time the live fire grenades went off incorrectly, it was due to the pin sliding out earlier than the sling design should have allowed. The plaintiffs then brought in another expert that simply showed that the grenade should not have passed QC with this fault. Lieutenant Ambrose testified to making Colonel Elmore aware of the faults and requested that the M87 be scrapped. He also recommended the US Army investigate Montegard for faulty design. Elmore had simply responded by sending through the requested report, but had filed it incorrectly where the Pentagon and Department of Defense never saw the paperwork. Elmore had testified that a clerical error outside of his responsibility was to blame, and he was remorseful for not following up appropriately on the request. Montegard of course rejected the notion that there was a fault and suggested that the soldiers were simply taking too long to release the sling to send the grenade flying toward its target. With the injuries and deaths reaching double digits, Lieutenant Michael Ambrose turned whistle-blower and went to the press and to the families of each soldier and suggested a lawsuit. Several attorneys jumped at the opportunity, and here they all were.

Charlie took a breath as the jurors lined up and began filing into the jury box. Twelve people would sort out truth from falsehood. Twelve men and women were charged with fairly evaluating the evidence, testimony, and information presented to them and rendering a verdict. The judge ascended the steps and the bailiff instructed everyone to rise. As one, the courtroom stood, with the exception of a few souls in dress uniforms who could not. The Judge ordered all to be seated and, as one, everyone took their seats again.

The Judge was an aging white man with a receding hair line. Well-kept white hair was neatly combed at the sides and rear of his head. He took his seat.

"Madame Foreman have you reached a verdict?" asked the judge as he looked up at the jury box. A middle aged Hispanic woman, wearing a black and white floral print dress stood.

"We have your honor," she replied. Her face was impassive.

Charlie braced himself. Everything came down to this. Oftentimes cases settled on the eve of trial, or sometimes even during trial after a piece of evidence had come out. But with their offer out, the plaintiffs had already invested time and money into the case and were determined to let it all ride to see what the jury would say.

"Please read your verdict," the judge stated.

"In the matter of negligence alleged against Montegard Arms & Munitions for the manufacture, production, and proliferation of faulty equipment, we find that the defendant acted negligently and even recklessly with little regard for safety and appropriate product testing," the woman spoke. The attorneys for the defense muttered to one another and Charlie felt his shoulders sag a little.

"Have you reached a determination of suitable compensation?" the judge asked.

"Yes, we have your honor. The jury believes the sum of 200 million dollars to be sufficient remuneration for the costs associated with the defective production of the M87 grenade," she stated.

Several gasps and quiet muttering voices were heard. Charlie felt his heart sink into his gut. Sylvia glared at her lawyers but said nothing. It was the worst thing Charlie could experience at that moment as a result of the trial. Even as the plaintiffs began to chatter, the judge rapped his gavel.

"Let the judgment be entered into the record. Counselors, if you have any appeals or motions to file, I suggest you do so swiftly," he said before dismissing the court.

Charlie sat in his seat, numb. A runaway jury, a jury which decided that the plaintiffs were not asking enough money or that the defendant had acted so egregiously that they needed to be punished, had just ordered payment ten times the limits of the policy. To make matters worse, the plaintiffs were originally willing to settle for the limits of the 20 million dollar policy, which meant that a court could later rule that the insurance company had acted in bad faith; and even that he, Charlie, had acted in bad faith. His phone buzzed in his hand and he raised it to check the text.

'Chicken Tikka Masala?' came the text from his wife.

It buzzed again.

His boss was calling him.

He got up and walked out of the court room. Before he left, he hit the green accept button. Several people turned to hear his boss screaming at him over the phone as Charlie winced and walked outside.

1

A month and a half had passed. The trial was over. The appeals were underway, escalating the case to the First Circuit court to appeal the jury verdict. There was some hope there, and that's why Charlie hadn't lost his job. But as he and his wife drove their little sedan through Bourne into Cape Cod for their anniversary, Memorial Day weekend, the words 'Administrative Leave' were on his mind. It had been three weeks and they were still going through all of his files, assigning them out as they put the Montegard claim with another adjuster in the office who would see the claim through the appellate level. Meanwhile his job was on the line. He'd banked a few weeks of vacation and so he decided to take it while they determined what would happen to him as a result of the colossal screw-up. It weighed on his mind as he drove along Route 28. With Montegard opened up to the verdict above the policy limit, they could sue the insurance company for screwing up and not settling earlier when they'd had the chance, which essentially put the insurance company on the hook for the whole verdict and then some.

The roundabouts opened up before them and Charlie sighed as Patience, his wonderful wife of eight years sat beside him in the passenger seat.

"Don't think about it," she said.

"Can't help it," he muttered.

"Well… at least try to think about something else. We're going to have SO much fun on this trip, Honey. You'll see.

And the company loves you. They won't get rid of you just for one claim that went bad."

"One claim that went bad that may cost the company hundreds of millions of dollars."

Patience sighed this time and reached over to pat his thigh.

"I love you," she assured him tenderly, almost apologetically as she tried to console him.

"I love you too," he said quietly in return. Charlie felt guilty taking this out on her. His wife was amazing. Patient as her namesake, demure, supportive, and soft spoken, she'd been his absolute rock as changes in management had come and gone. The company saw changes in personnel that happened all around him. Then, with a new manager barreling down on him with an apparent ax to grind, this claim had gone south, giving his supervisor all the ammunition they needed to put him on leave and investigate his claim-handling more thoroughly.

"We're going to have a wonderful anniversary trip," Patience announced.

"Yeah. Good food. Ocean breeze," he said with a light nod, paying attention to the cars before him.

"Romantic location. Pretty oceanside. Pretty husband," Patience said with a sidelong glance and a small grin.

"Yup. Yup. And, I am not pretty," Charlie said, giving her a ghost of a smile.

"Made you smile," Patience teased.

"Heh. So you did," Charlie said and gave her a more genuine if not apologetic smile before his prior anxious demeanor returned. This time Patience didn't interrupt his brooding.

Charlie had been distant of late. Their love life had

become far less connected than it had been in the past, far less physical than it should have been. Patience supposed some of it might be due to their growing comfort with each other as a married couple; and both of them being in their 30's didn't help anything, especially with Charlie closing in rapidly on the big 'four-oh'. But Patience knew that the real reason for the stress and strain on their relationship was the crushing weight of the leave Charlie was on. As the primary breadwinner in the household, Charlie's paycheck kept the roof over their heads and paid the bills, and her pay was often used as their retirement savings and extra expenses. Now with Charlie's continued employment being all but uncertain, they were already reconfiguring their budget. This weekend away had been planned months before the trial began, and paid for half a year ago, so they'd agreed to continue it at this point. But weekend getaways like this would be non-existent if Charlie's boss drummed him out like her husband feared.

They drove in silence until they entered 'downtown' Falmouth, a picturesque community of old shops, kitschy stores, and houses by the score converted into law practices, doctor's and dental offices, and architectural firms. Passing the occasional car on the road, the traffic was mostly made up of cyclists and pedestrians. Even during non-peak season there were more than a few people visiting Cape Cod.

Charlie figured that they were likely people like them, eager to enjoy the Cape around the open of the season, but with fewer people around.

Patience guessed as much too.

The car turned down a side street that proved to be Main Street and soon enough came to a beautiful mansion that had been built with a glorious garden in mind. The driveway was narrow, but one way, and the garden was impeccably maintained. Charlie followed the signs to the back; and in the expansive back yard was a gravel parking lot area. He pulled into the parking spot labeled Savannah, the room he'd reserved. Smiling finally, he shut the car off.

"Well here we are," he said as they sat in the car.

"So romantic. It's amazing how they designed the room to look and feel like the inside of a Chevy," Patience replied teasingly.

Charlie groaned and rolled his eyes, sparing her a smirk as they got out of the car and grabbed their bags. Three other cars were already parked there. A red BMW 7 series, a black Lincoln, and a small gold Toyota. Charlie popped the trunk and they got their bags and walked up to the back door where the guest registry sign was. The mansion turned bed and breakfast was actually built in a Southern style with a large wraparound porch that had been set up with chairs and small tables for dining, and chairs for lounging and enjoying the sunny beautiful weather of the summer.

The desk clerk smiled as they approached.

"Charlie and Patience Callahan, checking in," Charlie said with a professional if not friendly sort of smile.

"Oh, yes!" The young blonde woman behind the desk smiled and tapped an iPad on a stand behind the small desk. "Here we are. Savannah, right?" She asked confirming the reservation.

"That's us." Charlie said. Patience smiled and nodded.

"Great! Come with me and I'll show you around," she said and proceeded to take them through the ground floor of the large mansion. Breakfast, she explained, was fresh made each morning by the kitchen staff from a small select menu and served each day between 8 am and 10:30 am. The kitchen and breakfast dining area were on one side of the house. This was separated, she explained, by the main corridor. The main set of stairs just inside the front door led to the second floor where most of the rooms were. There was another staircase that led to the other end of the second floor hallway and also led down, as she explained, to the Savannah room. She then led them through one of the doors off the main corridor into a lavishly appointed sitting room. A small dining table for formal events and a wine cabinet with glasses and champagne flutes stood at one end of the room and a beautiful black baby grand piano stood at the other end. As was typical with such construction, a large fireplace dominated the interior wall, and large overstuffed chairs sat facing the hearth. Charlie nudged Patience and nodded to the baby grand piano.

"No," she said quietly. The clerk turned around and Charlie gave a smile.

"Is it ok if my wife plays the piano?" Charlie asked politely.

The clerk raised her eyebrows.

"Sure. Can you play, Miss?" she asked with a friendly and inviting tone.

"Oh well, I can play a little, yes," Patience replied modestly.

"Sit down and play something, Honey," Charlie urged and stood by proudly.

Patience sat down and adjusted the bench a bit before bringing her hands up to the black and white keys, her fingers stroking over the them for a moment or two. She pressed one or two to gauge the weight and then began to play the opening notes of the Moonlight Sonata. As she played, the room simply melted away as Patience paid attention to the instrument, and her fingers began to coax the melody and harmony out of the harp in the piano. As her hands and fingers touched each key and pressed it with the correct force to elicit the desired dynamic range, she wove the melody and harmony into the song she played.

The desk clerk looked on, obviously impressed as Patience continued to play for several minutes.

"Wow. That was delightful!" the clerk exclaimed with a smile.

"Indeed! Bravo!" Another male voice proclaimed from the other end of the room. A dark-haired man with a few streaks of gray peeking through here and there stepped forward. He wore a set of black slacks and a white polo shirt. "Mi dispiace. I am sorry. I could not help but overhear and came to listen. You play very beautifully, Miss." The man said.

"She does indeed," Charlie agreed with a proud smile as his wife blushed.

"Perhaps you would favor us with a small concert?" the man pressed.

"Oh! Well I mean I just couldn't," Patience said with a blush.

"Oh, don't be so modest," Charlie said with a smile and placed a hand on her shoulder. Patience smiled and looked aside.

"We could serve wine and I could get an excellent selection of cheeses for people to enjoy light hors d'oeuvres while they listen if you would like," the clerk informed. "It would be no trouble."

"I'm not sure. I mean, I'm sure people already have plans," Patience said with a modest tone, but clearly she began to agree.

"Madame, many of the restaurants are already booked

for dinner tonight with reservations. And those that are not are surely going to have lines just to get a table," the older gentleman said. "It would be quite wonderful, I am sure, for myself and our fellow guests to enjoy an evening of light music and refreshments," he continued with a nod.

"A-alright," Patience said with a nod, "I'll do it."

"Wonderful! I'll see to the preparations. Shall we say approximately 6 o'clock?" The desk clerk asked.

"That sounds wonderful," said Patience with a nod, her smile growing.

"Bene!" The middle aged man said cheerfully.

"You're one of the other guests?" Charlie asked the man.

"Ah, yes! Please let me introduce myself; Giorgio Scalfani. My card." He said as he pulled a business card from his wallet and handed it over.

The card read: Scalfani & Sons Investments, followed by the man's name and his address.

"Out of New Canaan eh?" Charlie asked with a smile. "You must do well for yourself," he commented.

Giorgio took his turn to be humble and shrugged with a simple smile.

"Well, thank you for the suggestion and your card. My wife, for all her bashfulness, does enjoy playing and looks for almost any excuse," Charlie said.

"Ahhh, well, we shall be thanking her for sharing her marvelous skill tonight. I am looking forward to a night of beautiful music," Scalfani said and gave a small nod of his head as he departed. The desk clerk smiled.

"Let's show you your room," she said and led them to the back of the main corridor to the stairs that descended into the basement and ascended to the second floor.

As they walked by the end of the corridor, Charlie looked

to the door of the only room on the main floor.

CHARLESTON

The door was slightly ajar and from within Charlie heard a familiar male voice.

"Yeah Mitch, this place is great! Thanks again for putting me up here. I'm sure the book will come along nicely and I'll get a good start on it in the next few days here. You know, sea air, quiet atmosphere, all that," the man said. Charlie listened and then noticed Patience waiting for him on the landing halfway down the stairs. He followed, and as he reached the bottom of the stairs, heard the door shut upstairs.

"Here we are, the Savannah. Now you have your own exit to the outside from this room, and the key works for both doors," the clerk said as she unlocked the room and led them in.

Charlie and Patience followed close behind. The room was elegantly appointed with a pale teal carpet and seafoam green walls with white trim. The large king-sized bed was well stocked with pillows and a down comforter. In the center of the neatly arranged pile of pillows was a small teddy bear with its own bathrobe, monogrammed with the 'S.H.' of Safe Harbor. In the corner a gas fireplace was built into the wall. The bathroom was dominated by the presence of a large soaker tub at one side and a massive shower that was easily large enough to fit four. Charlie and Patience marveled over the luxury.

"And here's your other exit," the clerk said with a smile and walked over to the side door of the room. It opened up to a small patio that was dug straight into the ground with a small decorative fieldstone wall. On the flagstones that made up the patio, a set of wrought iron chairs and a small table sat there for enjoying a bit of quiet in the shade of the wraparound porch that circled the house just above their heads.

"Now, the maids and I live in the servant's quarters on the back of the property. You may have seen the blue-gray building at the back of the garden when you drove in. That's where we stay. The emergency number and the guest wifi password are written on this card," she indicated and put the key down on the nightstand.

"I'll go get the arrangements started and inform the other guests of the concert tonight. Thank you again. It's so wonderful having entertainment here," the clerk said with a genuine tone as she left and shut the door behind her.

Charlie smiled at his wife and he slid a hand over her waist.

"Well what do you think?" he asked curiously and looked around the room.

"It's gorgeous!" she said with a smile. "But I don't have time to appreciate it if I'm going to get myself ready for the concert tonight. I have to work on my hair and take a bath," Patience replied and twisted gracefully and teasingly out of her husband's embrace as Charlie chuckled.

"Minx," he said as she scampered into the bathroom.

"YOUR Minx," she teased in return, and she stepped over to the bathroom to begin preparing for the concert.

2

Sylvia watched from the windows of the loft and saw the green sedan she knew so well pull into the parking lot. As the sun set further, she turned away from the window and began to dress for the concert. She wasn't really in the mood, but being cooped up like she had been was driving her crazy. She hated being cooped up. Even as her anxiety welled up and formed a knot in her chest from the stress of the last few months, she forced herself to slip on the little red dress she'd brought with her and straighten it out. She looked herself over in the mirror and nodded. She looked every bit the socialite she truly was. She stepped out of her room and walked down the stairs from the loft suite to the main floor.

Scalfani sat in one of the large stuffed chairs, wearing a nice suit as he sipped a white wine. A small plate of cheese rested on an ornate end table between it and another chair. He was speaking with a middle-aged man wearing a tan blazer with a black polo shirt under it. Off in the corner, Charlie stood by the piano speaking to his wife as she fussed over the music she'd found in the piano bench. There was a lovely assortment.

"Chopin? Tcherepnin?" Patience asked, clearly at a loss.

"Whatever you're comfortable with babe! I promise it'll be lovely," Charlie soothed her and gently squeezed on her shoulder as he looked over a piece of music.

"Nice, but trite. I just don't want to play stuff everyone's heard ad nauseam," she said softly. Patience wore a lovely green dress, one with a pattern of Celtic braidwork.

"Do you think anyone here has ever even heard of Tcherepnin? Chopin I mean, sure, probably. But if you play something lesser known, maybe not the Raindrop Prelude or something," Charlie suggested with a helpful tone.

"Well, who else?" she asked.

"I dunno. How about some Rachmaninoff? Some Dvorak maybe?" Charlie said.

"Shostakovich?" Patience asked, cracking a little frantic smile.

"Better wait 'til he gets sober," Charlie said, repeating a little running Victor Borge joke as he leaned in to tenderly kiss his wife's forehead.

"Mister Callahan?" Came a familiar voice. Charlie turned his attention away from his wife and blinked in surprise to see Sylvia walking toward him.

"Missus Montegard?" Charlie asked, recognizing her immediately. His eyes widened. Patience looked at her husband, to Sylvia, and back to her husband.

"Mister Callahan, this is the last place I expected to run into you," she said with a professional tone that flitted back and forth between being bemused and being irked at 'work' following her out here to this remote getaway.

"I wasn't expecting to see you either. Honey? This is Mrs. Sylvia Montegard. She was involved in that trial recently that the company was worried about," he said, doing his best to keep Sylvia's business private, even from his wife. "Mrs. Montegard? This is my wife Patience," he said, introducing the two.

"A pleasure. Your husband was... is, a very good insurance adjuster, even if his company doesn't quite think so," Sylvia said as she reached out to extend a hand toward Patience.

Patience looked back and forth between the two and set down a book of Rachmaninoff's work as she stood slightly to shake Sylvia's hand. Charlie winced a bit at the mention of being a very good adjuster. So, Sylvia Montegard knew what happened to him afterward?

"I didn't know you were the celebrity pianist," Sylvia said with a polite smile, turning her attention to Patience.

"Oh, I'm not a celebrity. I just love playing. My mother played the hymns at church and taught me how to play. The staff and one of the other guests suggested a concert if I was up for it," Patience explained.

"She plays beautifully," Charlie added.

"I'm sure she does. Well, I look forward to hearing the concert tonight," Sylvia said with a small smile as she walked away with a slight nod. She headed over to the bar where one of the staff stood by a bottle of wine and several of the crystal glasses, ready to pour.

Charlie smiled a little, trying to encourage his wife. Patience gave him a fleeting smile in return as she began to sort music that she'd found in the bench. Patience could sight-read well, and knew a wide variety of music from memory, but she had not prepared for a concert by creating a set. Charlie knew when his wife was busy, and after years of marriage, when he'd be more hindrance than help, so he gave her shoulder one last squeeze and walked over toward the rest of the guests assembling. A young, redheaded woman joined them now. Large glasses framed her green eyes and she had her hair pulled back in a messy bun. Wearing some clean black jeans and a black top, she was perhaps the most out of place among all of them. His gaze, and attention, however was drawn to Sylvia and after making his way over to the wine to fetch a glass for himself, he struck up the conversation.

"I didn't quite expect to see you while my wife and I were on our anniversary," Charlie said with a conversational tone.

"I didn't expect to see you while I was here trying to get away after the trial Mister Callahan," Sylvia responded.

"I think we covered that," Charlie joked lightly.

"Mmmm, so what brought you here?" Sylvia asked politely.

"I found this place in a little search online. Our anniversary trip is something my wife leaves up to me," he replied. "So I booked it."

"Ahhh, my father found this little place a long time ago. Brought me here when I was a little girl, along with my mother," Sylvia replied wistfully.

"Oh really? You must have seen a few changes around here over the years," he said conversationally.

"Yes. A few," she said with a polite smile. "I AM truly sorry to hear about what happened to you," Sylvia said softly.

"I wondered about that, how you knew," he said.

"The new adjuster said you were out on leave. I just reasoned it out. Bad verdict, you suddenly being on leave, and then seeing you here with your wife. Well, I managed to put two and two together," Sylvia said with a sympathetic tone.

"Well, thank you. It means a lot that you think-" Charlie trailed off and for the second time that evening his eyes widened in surprise.

David Elmore made any bit of clothing look like a dress uniform. The man could put on wrinkled jeans and a tee shirt that spent the night on the floor of a seedy motel and after a hard flinty stare, the wrinkles and grime would fall out of them so that they would look crisp and clean on his frame. Tonight, however he wore a teal polo shirt and some khaki slacks as he walked in. He held a backpack and a large green suitcase sat on the floor behind him, resting against the check-in desk.

Sylvia turned and her eyes flashed with recognition.

David flinched as he saw Sylvia, and let slip a momentary flicker of shock as he saw Charlie standing there with a glass of wine in hand.

"Well this seems like quite the place for reunions," Sylvia said, catching her composure first as she smiled and plastered on a cheerful demeanor.

"What are you doing here Colonel?" Sylvia asked. Scalfani and the other guest, the red-headed girl in all black, leaned forward to study the newcomer.

"Oh! Sylvia, I mean Missus Montegard, I'm just staying here for the big regatta over off of Nantucket this weekend. Have to 'up the blues' so to speak and support Hyannis," he said with a disarming smile. Sylvia smiled behind her wineglass as she took a sip. Charlie was fairly certain only he noticed.

"Is there something going on here?" he asked curiously, looking around and noticing a number of the guests and then Patience at the piano.

"The lovely Signora. She's agreed to play for us," Scalfani spoke up with a cheerful smile and raised his glass.

"Yes. We arranged a small wine and cheese party while she plays. I can take your bags to your room once we get you checked in," said the same cheerful desk clerk from before, leaving the wine. David smiled his agreement.

"That'll be fine," he said and headed to the desk with her to check in. A few moments later the bags were in his room and he was back downstairs.

"Quite a coincidence the three of us meeting up in this little bed and breakfast," Charlie commented once David rejoined them.

"Indeed," Colonel Elmore said with a sharp nod.

"Ladies and gentlemen, if you'd like to take a seat, I have, what I hope, is a selection you'll all enjoy," Patience said politely. Scalfani and the other gentleman shifted their chairs to face Patience even as Charlie and the others pulled chairs away from the dining room table to sit down, all facing the piano. Once they were arranged, Charlie and the rest settled in, and he gave his wife a little wink of support.

"I'll start tonight off with something a bit more familiar, a Nocturne by Frederic Chopin, Opus Nine, Number Two in E-Flat Major," she said politely as her fingers began to touch the white and black keys in sequence, each note weaving together in the air as they created the familiar melody and harmony. Charlie's foot tapped to the beat. Sylvia listened intently and politely. Even the out-of-place redhead seemed to enjoy the performance. The song filled the lounge area of the bed and breakfast and the piano created a wonderful atmosphere as the six guests sat and listened to her. A trill of notes and finally a slowing of tempo with a final chord signaled the end of the piece. Her hands lifted from the keys and settled into her lap. A polite round of applause cropped up from the crowd of people listening to her play.

"For the next piece we look to-" Patience began.

"I'm sorry. Am I too late to join the festivities?" came that same familiar voice Charlie had heard earlier talking from the Charleston room.

Like everyone else, Charlie turned to see who had joined them late, and his eyes once more widened in shock. Behind him, he heard a sharp hiss of breath from Sylvia and a muttered curse from David.

Michael Ambrose stood in the doorway, smile crossing his face from ear to ear.

22

3

As Ambrose saw Montegard and Elmore, his smile broadened and he laughed, stepping toward the two of them.

"Oh, now isn't this a coincidence," he crowed.

Montegard stared icy daggers at him.

Elmore fumed.

"A pleasure to see you again so soon, Miss Montegard." Ambrose smiled and extended a hand as he approached her.

She turned away and faced Patience once more at the piano, doing her best to ignore him. Ambrose smiled cruelly. Callahan settled back in his chair, but kept watching from the periphery of his vision. Michael walked in front of Colonel Elmore and snapped to a salute.

"Good to see you too, SIR!" Michael held his stern and crisp salute for a while before dropping it. "I suppose that's a little bit behind us both now, isn't it? Another life," Ambrose said with a smile as he stood before Elmore. "So what brings you two here? Two partners in crime getting away together?" he asked, laughing at his own joke.

No one spoke a word.

"I hope you enjoy the concert," he crooned and walked away, leaving the trio as he headed to the staff member who poured him a glass of wine.

"What's a man have to do to get a stiff drink in this place?" Ambrose asked with a laugh. The room was tense and awkward. Charlie felt his gut coiled like a spring and he forced himself to down the rest of his glass of wine.

A wave of nausea over the whole encounter, drowned in

the claret, rose up within him as the stress threatened to ruin his whole evening and the nearby imitation Persian rug.

Patience looked pale, flabbergasted by the whole encounter. But mechanically, almost without any sort of will from her mind at all, her hands lifted and began to play the opening notes of Rachmaninoff's 18th Variation from Rhapsody on a Theme by Paganini. The soothing tones began to wend their way through the air and seemed to draw attention away from what had just occurred. All eyes in the room focused on the piano and she continued to play the arrangement.

Michael sat down by the table and quietly spoke with the redhead. Callahan couldn't hear beyond a polite introduction. The girl's name was Angie. As Patience came to the crescendo of the piece, signaling she was near the end, Charlie's attention was fixed once more on his wife.

She finished and placed her hands once more in her lap. Sylvia and David applauded, as did Charlie, casting Patience a little wink from his seat. The Italian gentleman stood and applauded.

Patience blushed as she looked back to the piano, and her hands once more launched into a piece. Dvorak this time. Bacchanalia from his Poetic Tone Pictures. It was one of her favorites, and while it wasn't Charlie's, he did enjoy the way her head bobbed back and forth and the huge grin she got from playing it.

The concert continued as wine was served alongside a platter of cheese, which the inn's staff member brought around, offering small pieces for people to put onto their plates.

Wine, cheese, and music. Charlie was comfortable with the atmosphere, but was equally at home with a beer, a slice of pizza, and a little rock music. He wondered if Sylvia and Colonel David Elmore were like that too. Idly, he nibbled on his cheese as his wife launched into a Prelude by Alkan.

Another piece or two and Patience finished her concert, though Charlie knew she had a few pieces in reserve as an encore if she was pressed. As the listeners milled about, Charlie stood by his wife and quietly praised her playing.

"You're biased," she replied with a smile and a whisper.

"Not really. You were brilliant," he said as he offered her some of the cheese that was sitting on his plate. She delicately selected a bit of Wensleydale that paired wonderfully with the wine.

"You performed very well, Mrs. Callahan," Sylvia said with a smile as she came over to speak to her.

"You see?" Charlie said to his wife with a grin.

Patience blushed and canted her head.

"Thank you, Miss Montegard," Patience said.

"Montegard? Pardon me, but are you Sylvia Montegard?" Scalfani stepped forward to intrude.

"Yes," Sylvia said cautiously. Charlie and Patience remained polite, but silent.

"Ahhh! Bene!" He said with a smile.

"Giorgio Scalfani of Scalfani and Sons. I am very glad to meet you, Miss Montegard," he said, oozing politeness and glee at the same time and in equal measure.

"I'm glad, Mister Scalfani. I must apologize. Should I know your name from something?" Sylvia asked, perplexed.

"Oh, no no no. My brother and I are investors, you see," he said with a smile.

"Ah. I believe I know where this is going. Mister and Missus Callahan, would you excuse me?" Sylvia asked and walked off with Scalfani to speak quietly near the fireplace.

Elmore was chatting with the redhead and Michael stood by one of the floor to ceiling windows, looking out as the night descended on the Cape.

"Quite the performance. It was lovely. Thank you very much," the middle-aged man said, coming forward. He was the only one that Charlie hadn't met or been introduced to.

"Oh! Thank you," Patience said with a smile.

"I gather this was a bit last minute, but you play so beautifully, you'd never know it," he said.

"She certainly does. I'm Charlie Callahan," Callahan said, extending his hand to the stranger.

"Edward. Edward Whitehall. Call me Ed," the other man smiled as he introduced himself.

"This is my wife, Patience," Charlie said, introducing her. She extended her hand as well and shook Ed's hand.

"That was wonderful," Edward repeated his praise.

"So what brings you to the Cape?" Charlie asked with a smile.

"Oh! I won a contest at work. I'm in real estate and had the highest gross sales for the quarter. First prize was a trip to Cape Cod over Memorial Day," he explained.

"Ahh well congratulations! Did you bring your family?" Charlie asked, noting the gold band on Ed's left ring finger.

"Ohhhh, no. My wife stayed home with the kids, unfortunately. It was a trip for two but with my two girls at home, with basketball finals and exams coming up, they just couldn't get away. We couldn't get anyone to watch them, so my wife stayed home and told me that I should go by myself," Ed said almost sadly as he looked aside.

"Ahhh, that must be pretty tough. I bet you miss them," Charlie said sympathetically.

"I do, very much. Family's really important to me,

yanno? You work hard all the time to provide for them. You support them through everything, thick and thin," he said.

"That's how families are supposed to be," Patience agreed firmly.

Charlie nodded.

"To family. Here and the absent members," Charlie said, raising his wine glass.

A pained look came across Edward's face, but he smiled softly and raised his glass.

"To family," he agreed. Patience raised her glass and all three took a sip to the toast.

"Well, thank you again for the concert," Edward said and politely stepped away as if to examine the piano. His fingertips ran lightly over the keys, even as he didn't depress any of them.

Elmore walked over, the redhead with him.

"I must thank you, Mrs. Callahan, for a very lovely evening," David said with a crisp tone.

"It really was a beautiful concert, even if I didn't recognize all the pieces," the redhead said with a polite smile.

Patience smiled and nodded a bit to each one.

"I'm glad you both enjoyed it," she said.

"I'm Angie Harris," she said, introducing herself.

"Ahhh, nice to meet you. I'm Charlie and this is my wife, Patience," Charlie said with a smile.

"A pleasure, Miss Harris," Patience added.

"Are you here with Colonel Elmore?" Charlie asked. The Colonel gave a small chuckle at that.

"Oh no! I've only just met him tonight," she said.

"I'm here to try to learn to be a travel writer. See some of the big important places that everyone always wants to go. Write up the little sights to see, places to eat, things to do, that sort of thing. I'm looking to publish someday," Angie said.

"Ahhh, that's very admirable," Patience said.

"Yes! I was telling her all about the Regatta between Hyannis and Nantucket. The Figawi is going strong!" Elmore said with a brilliant smile.

"Oh! That's quite entertaining! A boat race, eh?" Charlie asked with a smile.

"It's been going on for decades. Gets bigger every year," David replied. "What brings you here, Mister Callahan? I haven't seen you since that awful trial business," he continued.

"A trial?" Angie asked.

"Er, yes. I was a witness in a trial recently. Mister Callahan was the insurance adjuster for the company that was involved in the matter," David replied, a little flustered.

"How exciting! Is it just as thrilling as on TV?" Angie asked, starry-eyed as she looked to David and then to Charlie.

"Actually, it's pretty dull. The plaintiff files a motion. The defendant files a motion. The motions are reviewed and either approved or denied. It's mostly procedure and sometimes a few witnesses are called. In this case, Colonel Elmore was a witness and had to testify. We met during the trial," Callahan said, playing the whole thing off as if it was a minor issue.

"Ohhhh, I see," Angie said with a polite, thin smile. "Quite a coincidence then, you two both being here at the same bed & breakfast," Angie pressed.

"Well, I guess it is," Charlie admitted and shrugged. "My wife and I got married over this weekend. In fact, tomorrow's our anniversary. So I booked this hotel months ago, before the trial even started."

"Awwww! It's your anniversary?! How sweet!" Angie cooed and squealed a bit.

"Anniversary, eh?" Michael asked as he approached. David bristled at the voice.

"Well we should raise a glass in a toast. First to the lovely concert we all enjoyed," Ambrose said and raised his glass. Everyone, including Elmore, raised their glasses. David gave a kind smile to Patience as he nodded his head. Michael sipped his wine, as did the others in the room.

"And a second toast: to love, and enjoying a romantic weekend here in beautiful Cape Cod. To both couples," Ambrose said, raising his glass and winking at Angie.

4

The room was silent.

Elmore stood there in shock as Ambrose casually drank to his own outrageous toast.

Ambrose smirked as the toast finished. No one moved or spoke as the echo of the tactless words hung about them.

Patience and Charlie looked at one another but didn't move to drink. Angie blushed and looked down and off to the side. Sylvia froze, her stare burrowing into Ambrose from off to his side. Giorgio Scalfani and Edward Whitehall quietly cleared their throats, hoping the small noise might break the tension.

"Hmmm," Ambrose muttered softly with a gleeful smile. "I seem to have hit the mark."

"And what do you mean by both of those couples?" Elmore asked with his jaw set, his eyes ablaze with barely checked rage.

"Oh I think you know very well what I'm speaking of David," Michael replied venomously, narrowing his eyes.

Elmore's hand shot out and gripped Ambrose's neck, jerking him off balance and lifting him into the air. Angie and Patience squealed as they scampered out of the way and Charlie backed up.

Charlie looked on as Scalfani and Edward both paled.

Elmore's eyes blazed with hatred.

"HOW DARE YOU!" David bellowed.

Ambrose struggled a bit as David caught him off guard, and with his hand gripping his throat, shoved him off balance.

Patience cried out as Charlie put himself between them and his wife. Angie scampered out of the way.

The staffer squeaked and froze in terror at the altercation.

Ambrose twisted in David's grip, shifting and trying to free himself even as his feet left the floor.

"Colonel!" Scalfani said as he and Edward stepped forward and made to grab for his arms. Elmore at first twisted out of their grips, but as Charlie stepped forward and put his hand on David's chest, Charlie's eyes caught Elmore's. David stared straight through him, his hatred boiling up inside of him for a moment more before his vision clarified and his gaze focused on Charlie.

"Let him go," Charlie said calmly, but firmly.

Elmore opened his hand and let go of Ambrose's shirt.

The former Lieutenant dropped to the ground, his knees buckling as he staggered to his feet and tried to keep himself from falling over.

"So I was right," Ambrose croaked out.

"Shut up!" Charlie said.

"Let me go," Elmore snarled.

"I wondered why you showed up here. Now I know. When I get done, you won't have a life left to live David. Everything you love will be gone," Ambrose spat out.

Elmore lunged, barely restrained by the three other men.

"I'LL KILL YOU!" he cried, murder in his eyes. The trio of Giorgio, Edward, and Charlie held David back as he struggled and Michael sneered.

Ambrose staggered off and left the living room to go back to his room.

"I think that's enough," Sylvia said coolly as she tried to

restore some semblance of order to the whole affair. David relaxed and the other three gentlemen let him go. "Mrs. Callahan, you are a marvelous musician, thank you so much for the delight of your performance this evening," Sylvia said cordially. A round of muted applause and a handful of 'thank you's' echoed from the various remaining guests. Charlie walked over to his wife and gently put his arm around her. Her frame was stiff and rigid as she did her best to force a smile. The emotional charge of the confrontation had taken its toll on her, and Charlie sighed inwardly.

So much for this anniversary being relaxing.

5

The guests filtered back to their rooms as the impromptu soiree ended. Charlie stayed back a moment to apologize to the staff member of the bed and breakfast. Why he apologized even he didn't know, but somehow Charlie felt responsible for the explosive behavior that had gone on that evening. He walked out of the living room area last and headed downstairs behind Patience.

She walked stiffly down the stairs.

Charlie touched her shoulder and she seemed to chill at his touch.

'Great...' Charlie thought. 'What a way to kick off our anniversary.' He gently moved past her to open the door to the room and walked in with his wife.

They entered the room and he locked the door behind them.

In silence, they got ready for dinner to make their reservations at 7:00. Charlie had booked a fancy little restaurant in nearby Woods Hole.

Throughout dinner, the restaurant's atmosphere was delightful, even as the tension between them grew with each passing moment. Leaving the restaurant after politely tipping and thanking the waitress for their delicious meal, Charlie offered Patience his arm. She refused it and walked beside him. As they got into the car, he turned the key and started it.

"What's wrong? Will ya talk to me?" Charlie asked.

"I didn't know you were bringing your work with you,"

Patience said, her tone full of hurt and embarrassment.

"What?" Charlie asked, a bit blindsided. He could understand his wife being upset by the drama, but her suggestion held an accusatory edge to it.

"This place is full of people you know. Full of that stupid claim that nearly got you fired! That might still get you fired," she said with a pained look as she turned to face him.

"I had no idea, hon! Honest! I made these plans months before the trial! I didn't know everyone was gonna show up here and be at each others' throats," he said with a grimace.

"I hated watching you deal with that claim," she said softly.

"Babe..." Charlie started.

"I went to bed and it would be hours that you were sitting up typing notes, staring into your laptop screen. You would come to bed and then wake up and sit bolt upright, panting and panicking over the trial. At the end of it, you came home white as a sheet. Then they said they were going to put you on administrative leave," she said with small sob.

"Patience. Claims are rough. It takes a special kind of personality to deal with it, and it takes another kind entirely to deal with it well and empathize with all the people involved," Charlie began explaining.

"I know, I know. And you're that kind of person Charlie. I know you're good at your job," Patience said, interrupting him before he could launch into his lecture.

"I wanted this to be a nice time for us, babe. I wanted this to be a good anniversary trip so we could reconnect, have some fun times," Charlie said.

"We could have fun times at home and we wouldn't have to reconnect if you didn't keep dragging your work around. Or following it," she said.

Charlie flinched and looked as though he'd been slapped.

Patience sat on her side of the car without a sound.

He put the car in reverse and backed from the parking space and drove back to the B&B in angry silence. They entered the room through the small external door. Being in the basement, they were the only room that had a private entrance and exit. He hoped that the ride had given things time to cool down. He had good intentions, but with his dander up, he couldn't leave well enough alone, and he knew he would say something he would regret.

"I tried, Patience. I tried to make this weekend lovely and nice and wonderful for us. I didn't know who else was showing up. It's not like I asked where people were going or what the guest list looked like. You know what? Yeah. I work hard. Maybe I devote too much time to my job, but I'm damn good at it, Patience. I take pride in my work. Every week day in day out I get compliments from my insureds and claimants alike who praise me for good decisions, for fair dealings, and for being honest and quick to answer the phone. I take all that corporate talk about integrity to heart and that means I pour myself into my work. And maybe I should pour that energy into you and our marriage. Maybe I should be a better husband, damnit, but, Patience, I'm sorry. The job takes its toll, and our marriage? It's… It's a refuge. A place I can come home to and not have to worry about my boss crawling up my back to question every single freaking move I make. It's a place I enjoy without fear and without having to worry about the stresses of the job. But when I come home and can't have that because all you can do is be upset by me working my tail to the bone, and blaming me for our marital issues and the stress in the household, all it does is make me even more stressed," Charlie snapped and lectured her.

He was met with a staggering sob, the kind that shook Patience's whole frame.

Charlie's shoulders slumped.

"I'm sorry, Patience," he whispered as she cried, facing out the window.

Long moments of silence passed and Charlie turned away from his crying wife. He slipped on his sneakers.

He needed to take a walk, let Patience finish her crying, and then he, hat in hand, well, metaphorically at least, would come back to her, kneel down and beg her forgiveness. He loved her more than anything, and he knew that the job was interfering with their life. He knew he had poured more into this claim for Montegard Arms than he did with any others. He knew that his marriage was strained because of it.

Most importantly, he knew his wife was right. He walked along the driveway that led to the parking lot in the back, and as he stepped around the side of the grand mansion turned B&B, he saw light coming from the sitting room. While the main floor was elevated from the ground, Charlie could at least see two figures in the room seated by the fireplace. As one got to their feet and swayed, Michael saw the light cross the features of a drunken Michael Ambrose.

Charlie walked along, heading down the driveway and walking down the block. As the rain scattered against the pavement, Charlie sighed a bit forlornly.

"Happy anniversary, Charlie. Here's the divorce papers," he growled to himself as he walked along.

6

The bottle turned over in their hands as they looked at the small vial of powder. There was easily enough there to kill a man.

"Damnit! I can't believe how easy this is going to be," the voice of the vial's owner spoke with a giddy tone.

"With all of those people here it's going to be chaos," they said cheerfully.

The bottle flipped up as the vial's owner caught it in midair.

"All my problems at an end, once they're gone, once this little thing is empty," they said.

Rain began to drizzle down outside. The bottle was placed carefully on the bed as its owner stood and walked to the window, watching as the rain began to darken the pavement of the parking lot. A solitary figure outside came dashing back across the parking lot, eager to get inside before the pitter patter of the rain became a downpour.

7

Michael walked out of his room, the last, it seemed, to head out for dinner. After the fight with David, he found himself hungry. With most of the restaurants in the area requiring reservations or several hours wait, Michael ordered a pizza for takeout and brought it back. As the rain began to darken the parking lot, he trotted back in with his meal and set up in the sitting room. It was comfortable, quiet, and out of the way of the main travel areas of the B&B, and he was eager to avoid any further altercations with the guests.

He stepped into the sitting room and set his pizza down on one of the end tables. A moment later he walked into the kitchen and returned with a small plate and several paper napkins. Coming back, he saw another occupant of the lavish sitting room.

"What do you want?" Michael asked tersely.

"After what happened earlier, I thought maybe a drink was in order. I came here to be alone, but we can share a drink." The other person said, holding up a glass in offer.

"Why would I want to drink with you?" Michael asked as he sat down and opened his pizza box, taking out a slice.

"Well I admit it's not like we're friends at all. But I didn't think drinking all of this champagne by myself was a good idea," the other admitted.

"Well… I suppose it *would* be a shame," Michael admitted with a huff.

"I'm glad all that ugliness is over," the other person said, twisting the cork out of the champagne. Soon two glasses settled on the table between them.

"I'm sorry for what happened," the other said. Michael sipped his champagne and nodded a bit.

"It's... a shame," Michael agreed.

"It really is. I wish all of that could be put in the past. Everything that happened," the other occupant said quietly and sipped their own drink.

Michael finished his, and set down the empty glass.

His companion stood and walked back over to the champagne, creating two more of the fizzing bitter cocktails before returning to hand one to Michael, taking a sip from their own glass.

Michael nodded and lifted his glass and swigged the thing back.

"Ugh. People actually LIKE this stuff?" he asked. It was his second.

"Supposedly they're VERY trendy. But they DO take a bit of time to grow on you," said his companion.

A small clatter of noise came from the kitchen and Michael craned his head to see if he could see who it was. He saw a figure ascending the stairs, but couldn't make out the figure in the darkened hallway as his companion enjoyed the next drink.

The pizza diminished and with each drink, Michael felt his head growing woozy. He dimly remembered slinging an arm over his erstwhile companion's shoulder and staggering back to his room to lie on his bed.

As Michael lay in his bed, the pain began, followed by stiffness and the soreness and nausea of the drinks.

As Michael Ambrose lay alone in his room, darkness robbed him of his consciousness.

8

Patience was a good woman. She cooked. She cared for him when he was ill. She kept the house for him. Every part of his life was better because she was in it. And what did he do to repay that simple kindness and that doting affection that she expressed in a thousand different ways, most notably by practicing her namesake virtue?

Charlie occasionally snapped at her. He ignored her on occasion. He went to bed hours after she had turned in. He ate the food she prepared with little more than a grunt when he worked late, and woke up before she did to head downstairs and begin the day afresh. Every step was a rap of his soles on the pavement, each one like the banging of a gavel on his conscience, marking him as guilty.

He knew she deserved better. He knew he was a rotten husband. His steps carried him down to the restaurant-filled main drag of Falmouth, and he passed plenty of restaurants boasting long wait times and a few with people standing outside in the rain waiting for a table. Charlie assumed that those places were some of the best in town. He couldn't see anyone waiting outside in the rain for mediocre fare.

Turning around, he trudged back and took an angled side street past the town green to head another block or so over. With every step, Charlie thought of his devoted wife and how wonderful she truly was. As he walked down the driveway to head back, his head inclined a bit to look at the sitting room. The light was off now. Michael and his companion, whoever it was, were obviously done with the room. A clatter echoed from the dumpster out back around the corner of the mansion, and Charlie thought it was odd that anyone would be emptying the trash this late, but headed down to his room to enter the room he shared with his wife. He twisted the key, entered the room and set his shoes off to the side as he slipped them off his feet. The room was dark as Patience had already gone to bed. Charlie slipped off his wet clothes and brought them to hang in the shower over the rack. He walked back into the bedroom, using his phone to make sure he didn't trip over the furnishings of the beautiful B&B room. He settled down in the bed under the covers and wrapped his arm around Patience.

She stirred. She was still awake.

"I love you. I'm sorry. I put too much into my job. I keep you on the back burner, honey, and you don't deserve any of that. I had no idea who was going to be here. I thought it looked so romantic on the website, honey, I figured there would be all sorts of young newlyweds and stuff getting away. I thought this would be just a nice and quiet romantic weekend. I wanted to reconnect for our anniversary to show you that I... I know I've been wrong. I know I've taken you for granted. That I've taken us for granted. I wanted you to know how much I love you and how deeply I care for you." Charlie poured out his heart in the darkness to his wife, his head pressing gently against the back of her head as he spoke and his warm breath flowing over her neck.

"I love you, Patience. Please forgive me," he said softly.

A thin graceful hand reached up and touched his own, gently stroking his fingers.

"There's nothing to forgive. I know you work so hard and that it must have been killing you," she whispered into the darkness. "I'm sorry too. It just came to a head and I let the anxiety get the better of me," Patience said softly.

"And I let the anxiety of the file get to me. I let it hurt our marriage and drive us apart. I promise I will work on that. I am so, so sorry, Patience," Charlie repeated.

She answered his sorrow by rolling over in the sheets and pressing her lips to his, giving him a loving, and forgiving, kiss.

9

The morning broke and the peace of the B&B was split by a scream. Charlie sat bolt upright in bed. The scream was right above Charlie's bed. He rolled out of bed and quickly stood as he grabbed his bathrobe and tossed it over his shoulders, tying it as he ran out the door to head up the stairs. There was a clamor on the staircase that preceded half a dozen others as the rest of the guests came down from the second and third floors.

One of the B&B staff dashed out of the ground floor room toward the front desk. The Charleston Room door hung open, left that way by the maid. The guests looked at one another and Charlie stepped toward the room. The last to arrive was his wife, Patience, as she came up the stairs to see what the cause of all the commotion was. As Charlie peered inside around the door, the grisly sight of Michael Ambrose's body lay before him. In a tortured, unnatural, and painful pose, his eyes were wide in horror as he lay on the bed. Charlie watched for a moment. His chest wasn't moving.

"What's going on here?" David asked, his authoritative voice bellowed as he stepped forward and elbowed past the other guests to join Charlie in the room. "What is all this ruckus abou-..." he began to ask, but his breath caught in his throat. His eyes went wide. Charlie noticed the reaction and his eyes flicked back to Michael.

"My God," David said softly.

"We should leave. Wait for the police. That poor woman is probably calling 911 right now," Charlie advised.

"Y-yes. You're right," David said, stammering at first as he regained his composure and turned to step out. Charlie followed.

"Mister Ambrose is dead," he pronounced.

A ripple of shock moved through the other guests as Charlie stepped up behind him.

Scalfani made the sign of the cross and raised his eyes heavenward as he prayed quietly. Charlie stepped around David and embraced his wife. She turned toward him, clearly shocked by the news. He held her as the guests milled about and after a moment, the maid came back.

"The police are on their way," she said. "They asked that no one enter the room or leave the premises." She tried to hold her frazzled nerves together.

Charlie nodded and he and Elmore herded the bewildered guests into the sitting room.

"We'll wait for the police in there. They'll likely want everyone together. It'll help their investigation if people aren't given a chance to go back to their rooms. That will narrow the investigatory field down quickly," Charlie said.

David nodded his agreement.

"What? But I'm in my bathrobe and nightgown! I can't be seen like this!" Sylvia protested. It was met with a general round of agreement. Angie shrugged.

"I'm good," she said plainly. In fuzzy pajama pants and a black oversized band tee shirt, she seemed to be ok with the proceedings.

"Some of us are used to more formal settings, especially when dealing with professionals. I thought you would be able to appreciate that, Mister Callahan," Sylvia said icily.

"I understand where you're coming from completely, Mrs. Montegard, but as long as the police need to investigate, we need to give them the freedom to work. That will go by a lot smoother and more quickly if we help them," Charlie said, trying to forestall a confrontation.

"We can suggest that they start at the top, with your suite Sylvia, and then they can work their way down. After they're finished with poor Michael's room, of course," David said. Charlie saw Sylvia Montegard's face slip from anger to a mollified indignation.

"Fine. If that's what's needed to get through this, then that's what we have to do," she agreed.

"Ah, scusi. But why would they search OUR rooms?" Giorgio asked. The Italian investor stepped forward and looked curiously to Charlie.

"Well, although we don't know cause of death, Michael was relatively healthy, so they'll likely make a sweep of the rooms and the area as part of a routine investigation until a cause of death can be confirmed. The police are very thorough in matters of death," Charlie said, recalling police reports and toxicology screens that would go on for hundreds of pages for what was otherwise a simple accident. Death sometimes meant the difference between 10 pages and 150.

"You mean this might be murder? There might be some foul play?" Edward stepped up and asked curiously.

"I'm not the police. I'm not the investigator. I'm just like you, but we'll let the police make all the determinations and give us the directions as they look into it. All I'm saying is that we should obey the law and let the police work, assisting them in uncovering what, if anything, happened. Mister Ambrose could have suffered a fatal heart attack. This could all be natural causes. We simply won't know until the police make that determination," Charlie explained calmly.

"Just follow the law," David echoed with a nod. "We'll all be fine." He assured the others with Charlie. As David gave a smile, the sirens became audible and turned into the driveway as several cars and an ambulance arrived.

Tromping footsteps echoed up the un-carpeted staircase of the B&B and the front door opened as several uniformed officers and a man wearing sport coat and jeans with a white oxford shirt stepped inside.

Charlie walked toward the front door.

"Hello officer. I'm Charlie Callahan. We're all in here," he said.

"Detective," the man corrected.

"Oh, uh, yes. Detective," he said politely and smiled half heartedly, stepping off to the sitting room with the others, leading the detective inside to the anxious faces of several members of the B&B staff and the guests.

10

The detective was a middle-aged man in his late 40's with straight, blond hair parted to the side. He seemed to keep it expertly combed and groomed, and sported impeccably manicured nails. To say that he was well put together was an understatement.

"Ladies and gentlemen, I apologize for any disturbance to your vacation. I'm Detective Martin Goodwin and we hope we'll be able to get underway as quickly as possible to clear all of this up. We have a lot of work to do, so I appreciate your patience and forthcoming cooperation," Goodwin said with a small but congenial smile.

"First thing we will need is the hotel registry to match each room up to each guest, and we will need to verify everyone's identity here as we investigate the area," said Goodwin.

"Why would you need all of that? Are we under some sort of suspicion?" Angie asked curiously.

"Not as of yet, Ma'am. This is merely routine procedure. We catalogue everything as we find it so that if something should come up that seems a bit out of place, we know where everything and everyone was and we can tie up as many loose ends as quickly as possible. Our goal in these matters is to process everything as efficiently as possible," Goodwin said with a polite nod.

"I can get you the registry, Sir," said the desk clerk.

"Thank you, Miss," he said as she showed him to the front desk and took him over to the registry to print him out a copy of the current registrar of guests.

The EMT crews stepped into the B&B, and headed to Michael's room. After a moment or two of attempts to bring him around, they called for the coroner and left, heading off with little fanfare. A county van showed up and the coroner stepped up the staircase into the main hall of the B&B before he headed back to Michael's room. Detective Goodwin escorted the coroner back to the room and they began talking. Charlie couldn't hear what they were saying.

Detective Goodwin walked back in, professionalism practically oozing from his calm smile.

"Ladies and gentlemen, as part of our investigations I would like to take statements from each one of you starting with the staff, particularly the young lady who found Mister Ambrose this morning," he said.

The maid stood, still looking a bit on edge. "Come with me, Miss," Goodwin said softly and smiled at her as he stretched out a hand to lead her off. As she approached timidly, he wrapped it around her shoulders in a fatherly fashion and led her off through the kitchens to a corner of the dining room.

11

Detective Goodwin interviewed the staff one by one, asking that each person interviewed be separated from the others under the watchful gaze of one of the uniformed officers. He took a moment to conference with the coroner before coming back into the sitting room.

"Ladies and gentlemen, as part of our investigation, I must ask you to surrender your room keys," Goodwin said with an almost apologetic tone.

"What do you need those for?" asked Colonel Elmore, frowning a bit.

"Just to complete our preliminary investigations," Goodwin said, trying to keep things as polite as possible.

"You wouldn't need our room keys unless there was a reason," Angie surmised. Charlie had been thinking that himself, but hadn't voiced his concerns.

A murmur filtered through the guests and Charlie kept his eyes on the detective.

Goodwin sighed a little.

"The coroner has reason to believe that Mister Ambrose's death is not natural causes. We also have information that there was a rather violent altercation between Mister Ambrose and one or more of the other guests. So we are, as of now, treating his death with some suspicion. Accordingly, we must ask for your room keys. If you choose not to comply, that's your right, of course, and I will get a search warrant. It will only delay things for what is otherwise a formality, but your rights are important to me," Goodwin said with hands folded. He looked at each of the guests in turn as he spoke.

Angie Harris stepped forward and handed over the keys to her room, New York, followed shortly by Giorgio Scalfani, with the keys to Norfolk. Charlie stepped forward third and handed his keys over. With Charlie stepping forward, Edward did the same.

David and Sylvia withheld theirs.

Goodwin looked at them both expectantly.

"I came here to avoid invasions of my privacy, Detective, so if you want to have your officers 'oohing' and 'ahhing' over my nightgowns and underwear, I'm afraid you'll have to convince a judge of the worthiness of your cause for a warrant," Sylvia said coldly.

"That's your right, and your prerogative, Miss. I'll begin working on the paperwork," he said in response and turned his attention to Elmore, now the lone holdout who hadn't given an explanation.

"Along with Miss Montegard, I think the law has processes and procedures. They're put in place for a reason. If others want to void those procedures by surrendering their keys, that's their choice. I say make the law do its work," David responded simply with a professional tone.

"Very well. I'll begin working on the paperwork and serve it accordingly. To those who gave me your keys, I'll begin our searches quickly and hopefully get this wrapped up soon," he said thankfully and turned to walk out of the sitting room, leaving the guests in the care of one of the uniformed officers.

The searches commenced, and the coroner finally wheeled out the body of Michael Ambrose and brought him down to the lab for the requisite testing. One by one, as his officers worked, Detective Goodwin asked the guests to give statements regarding the previous evening. When it came to Charlie, he walked with the detective and settled down in a wicker chair on the opposite porch outside, away from prying ears and those who had already been interviewed as well as those who were yet to be interviewed.

"I hate all this nonsense," Goodwin said as he grunted and sat down with a small smile. A cup of coffee sat there, one he'd been nursing all morning. "Can I get you anything?" he asked politely. "I'm sure we can rustle up some tea or coffee around here."

"Oh, no. Coffee and tea on an empty stomach make me a bit nauseous," Charlie said politely and sat down.

"Ah, well, I won't keep you and your wife is it? Patience?" he asked.

"Yes. My wife," Charlie confirmed.

Goodwin flashed a pleasant smile.

"We'll get you out of here so you two can get some breakfast. 'Lot of good places to eat in this little town. It comes with tourism, fancy restaurants and really good food," Detective Goodwin said cheerfully.

"I imagine so," Charlie said.

"So what brings you and the missus up here for this weekend? Normal tourist traffic?" he asked curiously.

"It's our anniversary. Eight years. I planned this weekend out to be a bit of a surprise for her," Charlie answered.

"Ahhh! It's really romantic up here. And congratulations on your anniversary. My wife and I usually head the opposite direction on our anniversary, head away from the Cape. We married in early July, so it tends to be a bit tourist heavy up here. We like to zip over to Boston or fly to Florida if we can get away," Goodwin chatted.

"Sounds nice. We live in Connecticut, so the Cape is a nice way to be away from home but stick close by enough that we can enjoy our time away from work obligations," Charlie replied.

"I imagine. Do you know any of the other guests?" Goodwin asked.

"As a matter of fact, yes, I do," Charlie said with no small amount of embarrassment. "In fact, my wife and I had a disagreement last night over it," he volunteered.

"Oh?" the detective asked, pumping for more information.

"I might as well tell you since you can figure a lot of it out just from the papers. Once you dig into my background you'll see who I work for and what connection we all have," Charlie said with a slight shrug.

"It would save us a lot of time, effort, and digging," Goodwin replied.

"I work for New England Federated Mutual Insurance Company. We're a mid-sized insurance group. Handle mostly commercial insurance and various accounts like that. I was an insurance adjuster on a very high profile case for our insured, Montegard Arms. That would be Mrs. Sylvia Montegard who refused to give you her key," Charlie explained.

"I remember that. A few months ago the jury came out with a huge verdict. Something to do with grenades?" Goodwin probed.

"Yes. Colonel David Elmore, the other gentleman who refused to give you his key, and the deceased worked together in the armed forces. They knew one another, and were part of the testing of a new grenade that was going to be sold to the army for deployment. There were problems with the grenade and the jury found Montegard Arms negligent," Charlie said with a small nod.

"So the four of you know each other," Goodwin concluded.

"Mhmmm," Charlie replied.

"Tell me about last night," Goodwin said.

"You probably already know all there is to know. Michael bated David into a confrontation and David shouted at him." Charlie said, summarizing the fight.

"You mean he threatened to kill him," Goodwin probed.

"Yeah. I think he said that, the sort of thing you say when you get really hot under the collar," Charlie replied.

"And now this morning, Michael is dead," Goodwin said quietly.

"Well, I mean, I don't think David killed him if that's what you're saying," Charlie said.

"You just said he told Michael that he would kill him," Goodwin repeated.

"Well, yes, but that was an outburst, a sort of angry bit of speech. We all say things in anger we don't mean, Detective," Charlie said, his mind slipping into a defensive posture.

"But he said it as a man trained to kill by the Federal Government, a man who had not only capability of doing so, but as he said it, it took several men to tear him off of Michael whom he was strangling at the time," Goodwin asserted.

"He got upset because Michael had bated him and egged him on. He was trying to get a reaction out of David and David got angry," Charlie tried to explain. He didn't know why he was defending David, but something seemed off about the line of questioning.

"I see. Well, tell me how you think Michael Ambrose wound up dead this morning," Goodwin said.

"I don't know. I didn't know he was dead until the maid was off calling you," Charlie replied.

"Hmmmm… Mister Callahan, I'll have more questions for you later, but for now please feel free to have a seat in the kitchen," Goodwin said, his characteristic smile returning to his features as he gestured to the doorway that led from the porch into the kitchen. Charlie sat down at a table inside as Goodwin began interviewing the rest of the guests, one by one.

12

One by one, the guests were questioned. One by one, their stories recorded. David confessed to losing his temper but swore he went to bed and did his best to forget the entire incident. Sylvia advised that she felt very upset by the entire affair and had gone to bed after taking a sleeping pill. Edward said much the same, that he was asleep and had planned to sleep in today and get a later start, hoping to catch a nice brunch. Each gave their stories. Each told the detective why they were there, to vacation, to escape the public eye, to enjoy the Hyannis and Nantucket Regatta, and of course Charlie and Patience spoke to their anniversary getaway.

Patience told Goodwin about the argument and Charlie going for a walk before returning so they could make up from the argument. Goodwin called Charlie to answer a few follow-up questions at that point and asked him where he'd gone, who he had been with, and what he'd done. Charlie explained that he'd simply walked down to the restaurants, had turned around and headed back up, describing his route. He explained it was raining, and he hadn't stopped anywhere.

"I did see Michael in the sitting room though," Charlie advised.

"Oh? Why didn't you mention this before? What time?" Goodwin asked.

"You didn't ask. You were busy asking about David losing his temper. And it was around, I don't know, maybe

8:30 or so. We had reservations at 7, left the restaurant an hour or so after that," Charlie said with a nod.

"Hmmmm... so around 8:30 you were leaving and saw Michael Ambrose still alive. That helps us a bit. When you returned from this walk, did anyone see you? Did you see anyone else? How long did your walk take?" Goodwin asked further.

"Oh, I don't know. Maybe half an hour or so? Forty five minutes perhaps? I guess," Charlie said with a bit of a frown. "No one saw me that I know of, except my wife. We made up from our little argument. But no one else I know of saw me," he answered.

"And did you see anyone else? Was Mister Ambrose in the sitting room at that time? What? Nine o'clock, perhaps ten after nine?" Goodwin pried.

"No, no one. The sitting room was dark when I came home," Charlie replied.

"Did you see anything else? Hear anyone speak? Any sort of information may be important," Goodwin pressed.

"No, nothing. I went back to my room and went back to bed," he said with a shake of his head.

"Did you go in through the back door or the front door?" Goodwin asked.

"Neither. I'm in the Savannah room right below the porch. We have a separate door that leads straight in and out," he said.

"So you don't have to use the main entrances to get in and out of the building," Goodwin surmised.

"Correct," He said.

"Did you leave besides your walk and your dinner?" Goodwin asked.

"No. It was the concert, a very upsetting dinner where I

argued with my wife, and then back here where we argued again, and then I left," Charlie replied.

"Thank you, Mister Callahan, once again for your cooperation," Goodwin replied and escorted him once more back into the kitchen. The detective left Charlie alone and headed back out to the porch outside. A phone call came in and he stepped off to the side, listening to the voice at the other end.

"I see. That's the preliminary? How sure are you?" Goodwin asked. "That sure...," Goodwin intoned and sighed heavily. "Alright. Can you fill out the affidavit I sent to you? I drafted it based on your initial reaction. Uh-huh. Thanks," he said and after staring at his phone for a little longer, he sent the correspondence he received onward.

Charlie sat with his wife, dressed now since they'd cleared their room. The rest of the guests were assembled after having been questioned as to their statements. Each had gone to bed. Angie corroborated Charlie's story about Michael being in the sitting room, mentioning to the detective that she had come downstairs for some tea. They'd all had their rooms and belongings searched, except for David and Sylvia, both of whom were still in their robes.

"Ladies and Gentlemen, I regret to inform you that this is now a murder investigation. I must ask all of you to remain here and cancel any plans you have until we can determine what occurred here," Goodwin announced.

A shocked look came across Patience's face. Scalfani made the sign of the cross once more and began praying softly in Italian. Charlie saw Edward's shocked look, and then saw David's face, a frown etched into his stony features. The frown caused Charlie to shudder. The look on Sylvia's face was no less panicked than how Charlie felt.

"Colonel Elmore, Mrs. Montegard, I have an officer on the way with a warrant to search your rooms. I'm hopeful we can have each of you cleared. I am hoping this is some terrible misunderstanding, and that none of you are guilty of this crime, but we have to investigate all avenues," Goodwin said by way of explanation.

"We understand detective. And thank you for your candor," Sylvia replied professionally.

The officer arrived a few minutes later and Goodwin served the warrant to Sylvia and David, stating that the officers had permission to search the entire premises which of course, would include David and Sylvia's rooms.

David nodded, as did Sylvia. The two proferred their keys to Detective Goodwin and the detective nodded his thanks, turning to head to their bedrooms to begin the search.

"The game's afoot, then," Charlie said softly.

"Game?" David asked with a horrified frown.

"Sherlock Holmes. Now there's a crime, and Detective Goodwin is going to start his chase," Charlie said with a slow nod.

Detective Goodwin was quite thorough. He and his officers set first upon Sylvia Montegard's suite, checking through her personal effects and under the mattress, and, as a courtesy to the staff, had their own maid on duty ready to clean it up when they finished.

The guest rooms still needed to be turned down, aside from Michael Ambrose's suite which was still full of officers from the forensics lab capturing trace evidence to record for the file.

They worked diligently in Sylvia's room to let the heiress get back to her life. He knew of her by reputation, and it never went well for the small towns that angered important people. He'd done everything she requested in getting the warrant, and once done, immediately moved to her room to get the search concluded. Soon the officers left, turning up nothing at all, and the maid began changing the tousled and messed up bedding, going about the work with a light blush as she changed the sheets and began making the bed up.

The detective and his crew moved downward to David Elmore's room on the second floor. Sylvia passed the group as they entered David's room and she made her way to the suite upstairs indignantly to change.

"Mrs. Montegard," Goodwin said with a light nod of recognition and deference as he let her enter the two floor suite. He and his men walked inside Elmore's room, and Detective Goodwin blinked in a bit of surprise. No one moved for several long moments.

"Officer Ramirez, would you be so kind as to bring Colonel Elmore in here please?" he asked. The officer working with him on the search nodded and he headed downstairs to retrieve the retired colonel. Bringing him back to the second floor, Goodwin stepped to the end of the second floor landing.

"Colonel Elmore, when we spoke, you mentioned that, after the concert, you were upset by the events of the confrontation you had with Mister Ambrose, too upset to eat, and so you went to bed," Goodwin recapped. "Is my recollection accurate?"

"Yes. It was a jarring thing to have a fight with a man who served under me for years, someone I regarded as more than just a fellow officer, but a friend as well," Elmore said with a frown.

"And about what time did you wake up this morning?" Goodwin asked.

"My usual time. Approximately 0530," he said, citing military time.

"And what did you do from then until the time you ran downstairs, as you are currently dressed?" Goodwin asked the Colonel.

"I got up. I made the bed. I began reading the morning papers on my phone, check the headlines, that sort of thing. Breakfast isn't served here until 0800 anyways, so I didn't feel it necessary to wake everyone up by clattering around and heading downstairs for a cup of coffee and breakfast which wouldn't be ready for some time," he said, frowning lightly.

"You made the bed?" Goodwin asked curiously.

"Habit of a lifetime, Detective, you get up and the first thing you do is make your bed before you go about your morning routine," David said firmly.

"Made the bed in the best of US Army style eh?" Goodwin asked with a small smile.

"Yes," Elmore replied.

"Thank you. Would you mind waiting back in the kitchen please?" Goodwin asked. Elmore narrowed his eyes before turning in a huff, stepping downstairs to leave the detective to his search.

"Officer Ramirez, please bring the maid from Mrs. Montegard's room. I have an additional question for her," he said and turned to enter Colonel Elmore's room. When the maid joined them, Detective Goodwin and the officers stood fairly still.

"Thank you, Miss. Now I must ask you, who on the staff has access to the rooms?" Goodwin asked.

"All three of us, Emily, Karen, and myself, Sir," she said in response.

"And whose duty is it to do the turndown service?" he asked.

"Mine, Sir. Karen is the front desk clerk and Emily works in the kitchen. She needs a room key if someone orders something special from the kitchen for breakfast. Romantic occasions and things like that sometimes require her to bring in and set up a breakfast for a newlywed couple or something, for example," she replied.

"I see. And have you been in this room at all yet this morning?" he asked.

"Oh, no, sir. I usually start with the ground floor, which was Mister Ambrose's room," she said.

"The ground floor? Why there? Why not the basement room, what is it? The Savannah? Or the suite at the top?" Goodwin asked.

"It's easier, sir. We come in the main floor to start our

day and go over the guests checking in and checking out. So I just head to the one on the ground floor first and give a knock since it's right by the staircase down. If I get no answer, I move on and return, but if I'm right there, it makes no sense to skip it," she explained.

"Sounds reasonable enough," Goodwin surmised with a small smile.

"Would you tell me then, does it appear that this room has been used or this bed slept in?" Detective Goodwin asked and gestured to the room.

The maid turned and finally noticed what he was referring to. The room was in pristine order. The bed, including the small stuffed teddy bear with his own monogrammed bathrobe, were in perfect order, just the way the turndown service set it up.

She shook her head 'no'.

"No, sir. I did this yesterday. The teddy bear hasn't even been moved," she replied.

"So no one has slept in this bed?" he asked.

"Well, not unless they made the bed before they left the room," she said with a shrug.

"And made it exactly the way you made it," Goodwin added with a light nod.

"Well, yes, sir," she said.

"Were you ever in the armed services miss?" Goodwin asked.

"No," she answered.

"Ah, where did you learn to make a bed like this?" he asked.

"It's a standard hotel fashion turndown. You learn it with your first job in this industry and you just sort of carry it with you wherever you go." she said with a shrug.

"Mmmmm, thank you, Miss... I forgot your name. I apologize," Goodwin said with an affable demeanor.

"Kaley," the little blonde chirped with a smile.

"Thank you, Kaley. We'll likely need you to turn down this room in an hour or two," he said with a smile. "We'll call for you to let you know."

She bobbed her head with a nod and turned to head back to Missus Montegard's suite, the Portsmouth.

"Colonel Elmore, I had you figured for a lot of things, but a liar wasn't one of them. Are you a murderer as well?" he asked curiously, his eyes falling to that bed, made perfectly in the hotel fashion. Nobody had slept in that bed. And if Elmore had, and had remade the bed, it would be in the fashion of his Army career. You didn't simply pick up a new style, even down to the throw pillows and teddy bear accents.

* * *

14

Detective Goodwin and his men began their search. Goodwin ordered the bed, especially, to be torn up. A man lies about sleeping in and then making his bed? It might contain something else. David was hiding something, he was sure of it. So when his officers came forward with a small glass vial that had been tucked away between the mattress and box spring, Goodwin sighed a bit. With a gloved hand, he carefully bagged it up and shook his head. He made a note attached to the bag explaining where and in what condition the vial was found. A small label on the vial had been torn off and likely cast away. He had a feeling Elmore wouldn't keep it on his person or in the room. He'd probably destroyed it a while ago. The scent was pretty remarkable. He wrote on the tag, asking the forensics lab to review it for what it might contain and asked them to cross reference it with the poison that had been found in Michael Ambrose's stomach.

Goodwin shook his head. As calm and otherwise dismissive as Elmore was, he genuinely seemed to think highly of the Colonel. First impressions aren't always the most accurate though, he reminded himself.

"Officer Carter, please bring Colonel Elmore in here," he said, holding the bag with the vial in his hand.

"Yes, sir," the uniformed officer said and turned to head to the stairs, going down to retrieve David and bring him back up.

Once again face to face, Colonel Elmore scowled at Goodwin.

"What is it this time?" Elmore snapped.

"Last night more than half a dozen people heard you shout that you were going to kill Ambrose," Goodwin began solemnly and quietly. "Your career was cut short. Almost immediately after the trial, you quietly retired with an honorable discharge. He ruined you by exposing some sort of incompetence or malfeasance on your part with regards to Montegard Arms and the new weapon system," Goodwin said.

"You've been doing your homework. So tell me what you want," David said.

"You swore to kill a man who ruined your career and forced you out of the position you loved and worked hard for all your life, a job you dedicated your life to as a career officer in the US Army. One promotion away from stars on your shoulders, one promotion from being one of the most important men in the country, and Ambrose stole that from you. If Montegard had worked out, that would have been a major feather in your cap and anyone could see you'd be on a fast track to promotion. Brigadier General David Elmore sounds pretty good," Goodwin walked Elmore through his thoughts.

Elmore stared back icily, a hint of fear creeping into his otherwise flinty glare.

"You swore to kill a man who is now dead of strychnine poisoning. And then we find a vial in your room, unmarked, that contains some substance that smells like strychnine. I am willing to bet that when the lab gets through with its tests, we will find that this vial contains traces of strychnine, the same poison used to end the life of Michael Ambrose," Goodwin said quietly as he held up the evidence bag with the clear glass container within.

"We found used glasses in Ambrose's room with a small residue. If all of those match the poison that caused the end of Mister Ambrose, we have means and motive," Goodwin explained.

"So what do you think happened? I told you I was in bed all night," Elmore said with a frown.

"You went to his room, maybe with a bottle of something, or perhaps coffee or tea. You allegedly tried to patch things up. You poisoned his glass and watched him die. You came back here to your room and began hiding the evidence or otherwise disposing of it. You didn't make the bed this morning. This bed was made up by the maid. This is how she does it. The habits of a lifetime in the US Army do not include rearranging throw pillows and small teddy bears," Goodwin advised. "We have a plausible opportunity. Unless you have an alibi," Goodwin explained.

Elmore froze. The look of a cornered tiger entered his gaze and he very slowly spoke his next few words.

"I repeat what I told you before. I was in bed… all night," he said quietly.

Goodwin sighed and shook his head.

"Then Colonel Elmore, I have no choice but to take you in for further questioning. You are not under arrest at this point, however we are holding you as a person of interest," he said softly. As he said this, Elmore's eyes grew wide, even as the cuffs slipped around his wrists. He was removed from the B&B and placed in the back of a Falmouth police car which took him downtown.

15

The other guests watched the officers bring Elmore down the stairs and outside of the B&B. Sylvia, Charlie, and the others watched in mute horror. Detective Goodwin came down a few moments later and cleared his throat to catch their attention.

"Ladies and gentlemen, as our investigation continues, I must ask that you not leave the B&B until we have concluded our investigation and filed formal charges," Goodwin advised.

"You mean you haven't filed charges at this time?" Charlie asked curiously.

"No. At this time, Colonel Elmore is being treated as a person of interest," Goodwin advised before he looked back at the group. "Thank you all for your cooperation," he added and turned to leave them to their thoughts.

Charlie sighed a bit and his shoulders slumped.

"Colonel Elmore, a murderer," Edward said softly.

"We don't know that yet, sir. We just know he is being questioned, which means they suspect him, but they don't even have enough to formally charge him and put the indictment before a grand jury to see if charges can be pressed," Charlie said.

"What does all that mean? Does it mean he's innocent?" Angie asked curiously.

"No. It means that they don't have all the pieces to the puzzle. They don't have enough evidence right now based on everything they know to charge him," Charlie replied.

"What more do they need? They must have found something in his room," Scalfani stated.

"They may have. But that doesn't mean much. Police only report on what they find, then make suppositions on how it came to be. Reasonable ones, mostly," Charlie said.

"You sound like some sort of detective," Angie commented.

"It's something I encounter in insurance claims, especially with cars. People rely on police reports to determine fault for auto accidents, but they aren't always right. Ninety-nine times out of a hundred, the officer comes on scene after the fact and just goes on their gut. Sometimes they don't even talk to the parties involved or any witnesses that may have been around," he said with a shrug, "but when we start getting statements and piecing together how the accident occurred and the scene where it happened, we come up with a different story now and again, a different outcome."

"So the police may have arrested the wrong man," Edward said with a note of concern in his voice.

"I don't know about that," Charlie said. There was silence from the others as Charlie sat there in the center of all of them. Patience's hand slid over his shoulders gently, reassuringly.

"But you could find out, couldn't you, Mister Callahan?" the imperious voice of Sylvia Montegard asked, her eyes fixing on him. There was a steely challenge in her gaze as he lifted his eyes and looked at her.

"Oh, I'm no private detective or anything. There's plenty of those in the phone book," Callahan said.

"But you COULD do it," Sylvia pressed.

"If he is truly innocent, yeah, I could probably amass

enough evidence to make the police look elsewhere, but I don't see why they should. They wouldn't have zeroed in on him if they didn't have a reason to," Charlie said, unsure, but his resolve not to get involved was wavering. As an adjuster, he had a certain sense of justice, of right and wrong, a certain sense that made a mantra in his profession that they 'paid what they owed, not a penny more or a penny less'. Even if that payment was nothing at all. One thing Charlie enjoyed about his job was defending people who truly were innocent from people out to get a quick payout from an insurance settlement. Did David have to pay for this crime? It was a crime. It was a murder. Someone had to pay for it. But was it David's fault? The wheels began turning in Charlie's mind.

"Very well. If he's truly innocent, why don't you?" Sylvia asked curiously. "Find the party responsible," she said.

Charlie nodded and then furrowed his brow.

"What's it to you? If he's a murderer, then why are you so eager to get me investigating this Mrs. Montegard?" he asked as he stood and squared up to her, matching her gaze.

"Because he's not the only one who wanted Mister Ambrose dead, or have you forgotten that it was my company that was involved?" Sylvia asked.

"I haven't forgotten," Charlie replied.

"David may have said he wanted to kill Ambrose, but Michael Ambrose was the reason my company may no longer exist. We're fighting even now to get that verdict set aside. If not for him, I'd be quite happy. Colonel Elmore would be on a promotion list somewhere in the Pentagon waiting to trade in his eagle for a star, and countless others would be better off," Sylvia said with a frown.

"Except for those who died," Charlie replied.

Sylvia glared at him, but said nothing.

"I'm willing to bet even you suffered. As I understand, your handling of my company's claim has been reassigned to someone else," she said. Charlie blushed in embarrassment. Sylvia smiled as her barb struck home.

"His whistleblowing impacted your career too," she said.

"And if we are being honest, my investments have not been de best since de trial," Scalfani said somewhat meekly.

"So you see, we all have a motive for wanting him dead. And if they can't pin this on David, they may pin it on one of us," Sylvia said.

Charlie looked around and nodded.

"Well I don't have a reason to want him dead," Angie said.

"Neither do I," Edward chimed in.

"That goes for me too," Patience said.

"Actually, you do have a motive," Sylvia said to Patience. "Perhaps one that is even stronger than your husband's." Sylvia cocked an eyebrow and smiled almost wickedly.

"What?" Patience asked, incredulously.

"Your husband's job threatened by a bad case thanks to Michael Ambrose. Your entire financial peace of mind, your household, possibly even your marriage, cast adrift so to speak all because of him. Perhaps you want revenge on him for your husband," Sylvia pointed out.

Charlie turned to his wife.

"Patience doesn't think like that," he said as he looked in his wife's shocked gaze. She softened as he spoke of her and defended her, "but if you can make that inference, so can Detective Goodwin."

"So you'll look into this matter," Sylvia concluded.

"Yes," Charlie said softly. "I'll begin looking into this."

16

The rest of the evening was spent as Charlie began to do research into the whole case. He began to categorize the evening, accounting for each event in sequence, the same way he handled claims, each event one after the other to the time of the murder and then the next morning. When he couldn't place anyone at a particular point, he placed a question mark beside their name and moved on.

He began at the trial and placed himself, David Elmore, and Sylvia Montegard there. Then, after a moment, he placed Patience there as well. She might not have been there, but she was present as someone who felt the effects. He went through the rest of the list and then placed Scalfani at the trial. As a financial advisor whose firm heavily invested in Montegard Arms, something Charlie found out with a good bit of searching around the internet, Scalfani was connected to the outcome of the trial. The trial lost the company money. The company losing money lost Scalfani money, and his clients as well.

Of all those people at the trial, Michael Ambrose, David Elmore, Sylvia Montegard, Charlie himself and Patience, as well as Giorgio Scalfani, all of them plus two more, Angie Harris and Edward Whitehall, were at the B&B. He then wrote down the reason for each one's presence. Again, where he couldn't fill it in, he placed a question mark.

Sylvia had family connections to the B&B which had been in business for decades, and her father had taken them here for many years on vacation. Heading up on the first holiday weekend after the trial made a lot of sense. The B&B equated to comfort and good memories, something Mrs. Montegard could probably use in the present situation.

Charlie himself had booked this trip before the trial after finding it for their anniversary. He'd even written 'anniversary' on their reason for booking when the B&B asked for a reason for the stay. He figured that the date of the reservation, sometime in mid-March, preceding the trial date, would give him ample enough explanation for why his trip here could not be considered anything but pure coincidence. Edward Whitehall won a contest and arrived alone because his wife and two daughters had other commitments. They did not wish to give up the prize he'd won, so he was here by himself.

Colonel David Elmore was here for the Figawi, a boat race between Nantucket and Hyannis that had grown bigger and bigger each year. Tickets were so scarce on the ferries you had to have reservations, and many places were packed with the tourists here for just that reason.

Angie Harris said she was here to learn to be a travel writer, to experience the big destinations so she could write about them authoritatively. He wrote that down, but didn't know whether or not he completely believed her.

Scalfani; he realized he didn't know why the man was here. Nor did he have a reason for Michael Ambrose being present beyond a suspicion. He wrote down 'book deal' with a question mark following.

He looked at what he'd drawn. Some connections to what happened and the events leading up to the point where Ambrose met his untimely demise stared back at him and he nodded slowly at his work. Now time to look at it the other way.

Michael Ambrose was poisoned. How? Poison of some sort. Venom perhaps? He realized he needed more information on the precise method used to kill Ambrose to begin making further investigations there, but for now he pressed onward. How did he become poisoned? Inhalation? He ruled that out as no one seemed to be impacted by it beyond Ambrose and the rooms weren't airtight. Injected seemed a bit of a stretch. Ambrose wasn't a drug user. He'd been a model soldier and officer at the trial and if it was self inflicted, Ambrose hadn't had the time to develop such a lethal addiction between the discharge a short time after the trial and now. Ingestion seemed the most likely option, as there hadn't been any signs of a struggle from his memory heading into the room and seeing Michael's corpse with his pained look on his face. But then what could Ambrose have eaten that none of the rest would have been exposed to? Again, he needed to find the actual poison; however, he was fairly certain that it couldn't have been something Ambrose would have ingested long before that evening. With the body's natural flushing system through digestion and the excretory system, he couldn't imagine that something potent enough to cause death would take very long to manifest some very serious symptoms. So if not the food and wine they all had a bit of during the concert, that left something he ate either before or after. Did Michael go out for dinner? Charlie remembered seeing Michael in the sitting room well after the concert ended and after he'd returned home from his own dinner with Patience.

What had Michael been doing in the sitting room? And then the question was, could Elmore and the others account for their actions and movements over the course of the evening? There were too many questions at this point for Charlie to proceed and that meant he had no choice but to begin questioning people in earnest.

* * *

74

begin questioning people in earnest.

17

Charlie looked over his notes. The critical piece he was missing was precisely how Michael had died. Something had killed him in a rather painful manner, but he didn't appear to have been beaten up or stabbed. Charlie and Elmore had both come into the room and found him. Elmore had been shocked. A man who dealt with death and spent his career learning how to kill and commanding men to kill others had been shocked at the sight of Michael's body. That alone was enough to convince Charlie that not all was as it seemed, that perhaps Elmore wasn't the guilty party.

Of course, Charlie reasoned glumly, Elmore could be a consummate actor. Knowing he'd be a likely suspect, putting on a shocked face would be a good way to throw people off the scent. The circumstantial evidence and Elmore's lack of an alibi certainly seemed to convince Detective Goodwin, but what had the detective found to directly link Elmore to the crime? Charlie left his room and headed up the stairs toward the bedrooms on the second floor. A police officer was stationed outside of Elmore's room as the last few technicians were cleaning up after documenting the scene. Charlie walked over and the officer stepped between Charlie and the doorway.

"Can I help you, sir?" the officer asked. His flat tone was brusque and unwelcoming.

"You might," Charlie said politely and nodded to the officer. The uniformed cop cocked an eyebrow.

"Sir, I don't think you..." the officer began.

Charlie whipped out a business card and handed it over to the officer.

"I'm looking into the exact cause of death of Michael Ambrose. My company holds his life insurance policy, and, upon my reporting in to the office today, they asked me to look into this. I was just wondering if you could answer a question or two for me," he said with a cheerful smile.

"I uh..." the officer said with a confused look as he read the card. "We can't discuss sensitive details of the case during an ongoing investigation," the officer replied.

"Oh, I know THAT," Charlie said companionably and gave the man a smile.

"I just wanted to confirm it WAS murder by stabbing. We already have a lot of the details. I just need to get things together," Charlie said. "I'll get the details and pass it along, then let the payment boys figure everything out when they write the checks," he said.

"Well, uh, no. It wasn't a stabbing. Your information must be wrong," said the officer with a shake of his head.

Charlie put on a look of surprise.

"Whaaat?" he asked in shock as he gave the officer his best bewildered stare.

"Some sort of poison. We found a little vial with white crystals," the officer said.

"Ohhhh. Hmmm. Well, this could complicate things. A drug overdose could be construed as suicide," Charlie replied seriously, gripping his chin between his thumb and forefinger. Charlie looked frustrated and pensive as he thought this over.

"Not a drug overdose. It was poison. Found dirty water glasses as well," the officer said.

"You're sure?" Charlie asked, looking and sounding

hopeful. "How do you know it wasn't cocaine or crystal meth?" he asked curiously.

"There wasn't a smell. None at all. Those have a faint odor to them that you get used to when you're busting people," the officer said.

"Hmmm… Well, I suppose I'll talk to the detective and go from there," Charlie said with a slight sigh of defeat. "Thank you, Officer," he said before turning away to walk back down to his room. White, odorless, crystalline powder. Ingested. Causing immense pain and suffering. Now to find out what did it.

Charlie walked down the stairs to his room and opened his laptop. Typing in a list of characteristics given away by the officer, he began searching for poisons that matched those characteristics. Of course without lab reports and forensic facilities at his fingertips, he couldn't exactly be sure; but as he matched each characteristic, starting with the color, then the crystalline nature of the powder, followed by the odorless characteristic, it narrowed his search down considerably. Searching through those, he found one that made his blood run cold. Strychnine. The description he read regarding it stated specifically that it caused asphyxiation with great pain approximately an hour after ingestion or otherwise being taken into the body. He thought back to how Michael looked when he and David discovered him on the bed. Twisted and contorted with pain as he was, Charlie couldn't imagine what brought about such a result. As he reviewed the symptoms, painful muscle spasms, asphyxiation, rigid jaw, arm, and leg joints, and uncontrollable arching of the neck and back, it simply clicked into place.

Charlie sighed as he shut the laptop and needed to think. There was something wrong about this. One of the other characteristics of strychnine was the terribly bitter taste. He couldn't imagine that Michael would take it willingly. Something had to mask the flavor. Water wouldn't do it, and he couldn't imagine Michael wouldn't call 911. Something had to prevent him from calling for help and from detecting the poison in the first place.

He needed to think, and that meant a cup of coffee. Making his way up from his basement room, he headed to the kitchen.

18

Making his way to the kitchen, Charlie grabbed a mug and headed to the little instant single-cup coffee maker. It wasn't the best coffee in the world, but it would suffice. Mediocre coffee, after all, was better than no coffee at all. The little machine hissed and sputtered out the final few drops of the bitter black liquid as Charlie thought about the sequence of events. He walked over to sit on one of the stools by the breakfast bar.

"Oh! I didn't know anyone else was in here. I'm sorry," a woman's voice chirped.

Charlie looked over to the side, his eyes catching the shock of red hair. Angie Harris, one of the other guests of the B&B entered the kitchen.

"Oh, you're not intruding or anything. And if we're all together locked down like this, we're going to have to get comfortable," Charlie replied with a forced smile.

Angie pulled out her phone and sat down around the corner of the breakfast bar and began typing on the device.

"This whole thing is silly you know," she said with a cocked eyebrow as she looked over at Charlie.

He paused mid sip and looked at her.

"Oh?" he asked curiously.

"Yeah. See there's one thing the cops don't know," Angie said.

"What's that?" Charlie asked curiously.

"David wasn't the last one to see Michael alive," she said cockily, raising an eyebrow suggesting she knew even more than that.

"Why haven't you told the police this?" Charlie asked her.

"Because they're going to chase the obvious rabbit trail. Man whose career is ruined by Michael threatens openly to kill him and assaults him in front of witnesses. It's the perfect suspect to chase. But he's not the last one Michael was with. I heard Michael talking to someone late last night," Angie said with a smile.

"That doesn't answer why YOU haven't told the police," Charlie said.

"They don't want to know. They didn't ask. They just kept hounding on David. But I think they'll change their minds soon enough," Angie said with a grin.

"Change their minds?" he probed further.

"Yeah. I figure once they realize someone else was with Michael after the Colonel went to bed, they'll be eager to follow up on that, and THAT is where the news is." Angie said with a snicker.

"News? I thought you were a travel writer," he replied.

"Oh, well, yeah. I mean that's how I want to get my start in REAL journalism. Write puff pieces that get picked up by major news, then start working on harder more difficult stories. I can't think of anything juicier that I can use to prove myself than being on the inside of a murder investigation as it happens. Reporting from the inside like this NEVER happens," Angie gushed with a bright, almost manic grin.

"I think you should be careful what you wish for. The police may not want details of the case released to the public in case the killer had friends on the outside. Friends who might go to ground, destroy evidence, that sort of thing," Charlie said and took another sip of his coffee.

"Oh, I won't do anything STUPID, but this is too good of an opportunity to pass up," she said with a smile.

"So if David wasn't the last one to see Michael alive, who was?" Charlie asked her, trying to pry what she knew out of her.

"Oh, I couldn't tell you that, Mister Callahan. If I did, you might run to the police and ruin the whole story," she said with a grin. "But rest assured, I'll tell the police everything I know. See, that night when Michael was having pizza, I came to get a late night cup of tea. I walked past the doorway to the sitting room where your wife gave her concert, where Michael was eating his meal. That was well after the confrontation and after David allegedly went off to bed. The person with Michael in that room was definitely not the Colonel," she said with a bright and tantalizing smile.

Charlie was dumbstruck. It wasn't an alibi, but it shook the theory the police were working off of and actually helped to click a few more pieces of the puzzle into place for him. He looked at Angie and gave a slow nod.

"Well... you just be careful," he said quietly and took the rest of his coffee out of the kitchen and headed back to his room downstairs. He flipped open the laptop and began scanning and reviewing his notes, watching as the words in his little web outline began to connect. Angie knew something. She wasn't saying what she knew, but she knew something that could exonerate David. But then, if David hadn't done it, that left the question of who did?

Montegard? Scalfani? Whitehall? Or was it even Angie herself trying to divert suspicion? Charlie needed to get some fresh air with this. Patience sat on the bed and looked up from her book that she was reading.

"Is everything all right?" she asked.

"Yeah, honey. I, uh, I think I may be getting somewhere on this," Charlie said with a slight frown. He didn't want to get too far ahead of himself. Patience shut the book and set it aside.

"What is it?" she pressed.

"I don't know, but one of the guests is hiding a secret, something other than just who murdered Michael, but more importantly perhaps, why," he said, and his tone of voice quavered at the realization.

Charlie stood alone in the room. Before him on the bed, Michael was twisted and gnarled by the poison that had rushed through his body causing painful spasms and labored breathing. The muscle contractions that had finally killed him turned his body into a grotesque parody of the human form. A rasping breath rattled through Michael's snarl of pain.

"Guilty," the jaw rattled and creaked as the breath hissed out of the corpse on the bed.

"Guilty all," the corpse said once more as it began to rise from the bed with a creaking and bone-popping noise that echoed like the rapid beat of a snare drum in his mind.

"GUILTY!" The terrible scream echoed and Charlie shot bolt upright in bed, panting in the dark room.

"Charlie!" Patience woke up with him. "Are you ok, honey?" she asked in a near panic.

Charlie panted and tried to catch his breath.

"Yeah… Yeah I'm fine," he began to assure her.

"Do you need me to call 911?" she asked, turning over to turn on the light and grab her phone, ready to dial an ambulance.

"No. No, honey. I just had a terrible… a terrible nightmare," he said and caught his breath finally as his short panting gasps turned into a long drawn out deep breath and a sigh as he fell back against the bed.

"Do you want to talk about it?" Patience leaned over her husband and pressed her hand to his chest, looking at him, her brow knit in concern as she searched his face. Her eyes darted here and there as if somehow the answers to her husband's anxieties might be written in the grey hairs or his own crow's feet.

"It was everything that was going on; seeing Michael's… body," he said quietly after several long moments. "It was haunting and terrible. I've seen injuries. I've seen fatality reports. I've seen surgical photos. Discovering a dead man like that was, something new," he told her. His arm curled around his wife's back and he held her close. She laid her head on his shoulder and he pressed a kiss softly to her forehead as they held close to one another.

While Patience's breathing slowed to indicate she went back to sleep, he never did. He simply rested with her in the crook of his arm with her head on his chest, tenderly embracing her husband as they slept side by side.

As dawn filtered through the blinds in the room's smaller windows, he waited to leave the serenity of the bed and his wife's embrace for a while. Finally rolling gently out from her arms, he stood and went to freshen up so he could head upstairs for coffee.

The hot water of the shower helped wake him up and wash away the remnants of his nightmare.

As the bathroom steamed up, his mind thought back over the events of the last few days, what was said, what was discovered.

Michael Ambrose was killed by strychnine poisoning. It wasn't inhaled as far as he was aware, and the investigation suggested that it was ingested, possibly by the dirty glasses they found in his room.

Colonel David Elmore had very publicly and very loudly sworn to kill Michael. After that, he was caught in a lie. He'd said he had gone home to bed, but he hadn't. And then there was the vial of the powder that they found in his room.

Then there was Angie's revelation in the kitchen yesterday. She'd heard someone else, someone whose voice she didn't recognize, but someone other than David Elmore in the sitting room with Michael before he died. That matched up to what he himself saw when he went on his evening walk: a light on, and shadows moving in the sitting room.

A couple of things struck Charlie as odd. Strychnine, from all his research, had a very bitter taste to it. So how did Michael ingest it without knowing? How did David get the poison into the glass? And after he did it, why would he have not gone back to bed? If his alibi was to claim he'd been in bed all night, the best thing to do would be to go to sleep. And of course, if he was going to kill him with something like poison, announcing his intent to kill Michael was the worst thing he could have done!

The more Charlie thought about this, the less it made sense. There were too many things that didn't add up, too many unanswered questions. If David DID all of this, where had he spent the night? How had he gotten Michael to drink the strychnine? And why hide the evidence in his own room if he was there in Michael's bedroom that very night? Wouldn't it have been better to wipe the vial, leave it in Michael's room, and go back to his own room and sleep? If he had, there would be nothing substantial to connect him to the crime itself.

Charlie got out of the shower and toweled off. He finished his morning shave and then opened his suitcase to pull out his clothes for the day: a set of khaki shorts and a white button down cotton shirt he'd leave untucked and unbuttoned over a grey tee shirt. Simple clothes for a day of working and poring over the whole case again.

His gaze turned to the bed he and Patience shared, and he smiled as he saw her beautiful form half covered by the blankets. His eyes took on a gentle gaze as he took in how lucky he was to have her as his wife, sharing his bed.

Charlie's mind twisted and something in his head clicked. His eyes widened in realization and he dashed for the door.

Patience jerked awake and called after him, startled awake, but he didn't stop. He was already dashing up the stairs.

20

Charlie raced up the stairs to the ground floor and rounded the banister to head up to the second floor just as Sylvia Montegard was exiting her room in a flowery sun dress.

"Missus Montegard!" Charlie hailed her and trotted down the hallway of the second floor toward her, panting a bit from his sprint up the stairs.

She turned as she finished locking her door, blinking in surprise at the panting and flushed Charlie Callahan.

"Mister Callahan, whatever is the matter?" she asked, confused and a bit perplexed.

"We have to talk about David. Now!" he replied tersely.

"About Colonel Elmore? What about him?" Sylvia asked, shaking her head as she tried to understand. "Have you uncovered something that could exonerate him?" she asked, her interest piqued.

"I have. And I want to know why you didn't tell the police about his alibi," Charlie said.

Sylvia was flabbergasted by the whole assertion.

"What do you mean?" she asked, meeting his gaze. Charlie glared at her with a cold stare.

"I mean, I want to know why you didn't tell the police he was sharing your bed the night that Ambrose was murdered," he said in a low voice.

Sylvia's eyes flew wide with shock and she said nothing for several long moments, the very words taken straight away from her by the accusation.

Then her gaze shifted and her face changed as the

surprised and shocked look dissipated.

"Fine. Come with me," she said quietly and unlocked her room door and headed inside.

Charlie gave a glance over his shoulder and then turned back to follow her inside.

Sylvia stood inside her room and shut the door behind Charlie once he joined her. She stepped over toward her bureau where a small wristlet purse resided. She unzipped the purse and pulled out an antique silver cigarette case, taking one of the cigarettes out along with a lighter. A few flicks of the lighter and the little flame kissed the tip of the cigarette as Sylvia set the lighter down and took a drag.

Suddenly, the heiress seemed to change in front of Charlie. Her earlier poise and icy attitude that was meant to keep people at bay dropped away as she regarded him.

"Why should I confirm or tell you anything?" Sylvia asked, bitterness lacing her tone.

Charlie was caught off guard by the question.

"Because... you asked me to look into this in the first place!" he responded, a bit flabbergasted. "You wanted me to investigate the whole thing. You made a big show about how I had a motive, and you could have a motive, even my wife could have a motive! But you still asked me to see if I could prove David innocent, or punch enough holes in Detective Goodwin's theory to make him start sniffing around elsewhere," Charlie said, stepping toward her as his tone grew harsher with conviction entering his voice.

"Yes. I did. I did NOT ask you to go making wild accusations and casting aspersions about my character!" Sylvia snapped back.

"How wild is it? You and David knew each other professionally. The M87 project required you two to work together closely. Both of you show up here after the trial. Michael Ambrose winds up dead, and David says he was in bed, but his bed was perfectly made and nobody had slept in it. Elmore swore publicly that he'd kill Michael, but that was a moment of passion. The vial the police found was something planned and pre-purchased, and Elmore wouldn't have left it lying around, but there it was, under a perfectly made bed, not made in the style of a career Army officer, but in the style of a housemaid," Charlie explained and laid everything out, taking another step toward Sylvia. "So David lies to the police, saying he was in bed all night, why? To cover up where he TRULY was!"

"Fine. So he might have been sleeping with someone else. Maybe that… that… Angie girl! She could have been sleeping with David," Sylvia surmised and gesticulated, even as her eyes widened a bit. She didn't even believe her own supposition.

"It's the 21st Century, Missus Montegard. If two single people were sleeping with each other, they'd simply tell the police the truth, and that would give David all the alibi he needed, yet neither David nor Angie said a word to that effect. No, David was not in his bed, but he was sleeping elsewhere. It wasn't with Angie. She would have spoken up, and so would the Colonel. That leaves you, Mr. Scalfani, and Mr. Whitehall. Mr. Scalfani is devoutly Catholic, and married, and Mr. Whitehall is married with several children himself. While these in and of themselves are no guarantees, it's far more likely that he was sleeping with someone he knew well, someone that he was close to. This someone would be someone that could match his personality and was in such a position that Elmore wouldn't even let the whiff of scandal arise from sleeping with them, particularly if they're married," Charlie said, laying out his trail of premises, each one building on the last. "I doubt it's either Scalfani or Whitehall, but you on the other hand would fit very nicely into that situation. Your company is already in trouble. Your marriage is known to be rocky, at best, so you carry out an affair with the crisp, mature US Army officer. Your marriage and your company's reputation are up in the air though; and beyond that, if anyone knew of your association as lovers, the conflict of interest would ensure that the Army would almost certainly not have even bothered with the M87 design. If they did, they would have arranged different testing grounds and a different officer overseeing it all. But with your lover overseeing the testing, the flaws could get buried. The problem reports could get simply lost in the massive bureaucracy of the Department of Defense, and that would give Montegard Arms time to work out the flaws on your own without pesky reports making their way to the public and tanking your stock prices, depriving your company of who knows how much? Tell me if I'm wrong, Sylvia," Charlie said, fixing her with an intense stare.

Sylvia remained silent and flicked her cigarette over an ash tray on the bureau. She narrowed her gaze and clicked her tongue against her teeth.

"Alright. So we slept together. He was here giving me more passion in one hour than I've gotten out of months, no, YEARS of my marriage!" Sylvia spat venomously.

"And all that cost the two of you were a few lives of a few American soldiers," Charlie said quietly.

Sylvia flushed and looked down.

"I didn't want that to happen. You remember, I was eager to pay the families something, eager to apologize."

"I remember. I don't condone what you did, any of it at all, in fact! But, as long as David was sleeping with you, he was not murdering Michael Ambrose and hiding a vial of Strychnine in his bedroom," Charlie reasoned.

"He didn't want to tarnish my reputation," she said quietly, her voice choking up a bit as smoke curled up her arm from the cigarette. Another flick kicked ash off the end as she drew in a ragged breath, tears forming in her eyes.

"The best way to prove David's innocence is for you to come forward, and admit what happened."

"I can't do that," Sylvia said quietly. "Don't you think I want to? Don't you think I love David? That I want him to walk free? To be with me again? But if that happens, I lose everything, and so does he."

Charlie stood in her room, crossing his arms over his chest as he thought in silence. A few moments passed with the only sound between them coming from her intermittent sobs as Sylvia cried from the cathartic release of the secrets she'd been keeping for so long.

"I'll keep this a secret, for now," Charlie said quietly.

Sylvia looked up, her eyes glistening with a little hope.

"If I can prove David innocent by other means, I will. And then I'm going to talk to David later about coming clean and turning yourselves in for any criminal charges that may await you two. Your affair cost people their lives, and there has to be an answer for that," Charlie said with a hard stare.

Sylvia mutely nodded.

Charlie turned and left her there to her thoughts.

He had solved one part of the whole mystery: the police had the wrong guy. All David had to do was open his mouth and have Sylvia confirm what Charlie had just laid out before her. David would walk free, and then the police would have the same problem that Charlie now faced: if David didn't kill Michael, who did?

Charlie stepped down the stairs as he reflected on this and shoved his hands in his pockets.

His feet took him toward the back door. The officer stationed there held up a hand to stop Charlie.

"Sorry, Officer, I just need a little fresh air. I just wanted to step outside," Charlie said. The officer looked Charlie over and studied him for a moment before nodding and stepping to the side. Charlie walked out and stepped down the stairs to walk down to the driveway and followed it toward the front of the house. As his feet carried him through the beautiful gardens out front, his mind turned things over and over trying to come up with a new angle.

It seemed to Charlie he was at least one step ahead of the police, even if David confessed to the affair and cleared his name.

"At least I know I didn't do it," he said, chuckling at his own macabre joke.

21

The list of suspects was shifting and it appeared to narrow. At least if Sylvia and David confessed to his supposition, then the suspect list would narrow by two. Charlie walked through the parking lot and his shoes crunched over gravel as he shoved his hands in his pocket. Some vacation this turned out to be. He looked around and his eyes took in the pretty floral arrangements along the driveway. The petunias and geraniums planted with ferns and hosta were picture perfect and well manicured. They were interspersed with tulips and mums and peonies so that whenever the flowers were blooming, there would always be color in the garden beds. Charlie walked along the edge of the garden and thought to himself, mulling over the facts of the case. David could still have committed the murder, he realized. With Sylvia providing an otherwise airtight alibi for his whereabouts for the evening, and he for her, he could have sneaked out, poisoned Michael Ambrose, and walked right back, nice as you please, up to Sylvia's room. Of course, for the sake of the scandal to Sylvia's marriage and public presence, he would lie; but over the course of the investigation, and under interrogation, he'd quietly let slip that he was Sylvia Montegard's lover. She would discretely confirm it to the police. The police would release David Elmore, explaining that he had an alibi; and perhaps, with a legal document or two, that part of the case could be sealed away for privacy's sake. Sometimes privacy was a commodity in the justice world, and a good lawyer could

93

purchase that privacy for a retainer fee and a reasonable hourly billing rate.

The stones crunched beneath the soles of his shoes as his steps carried him along. The whole affair with David and Sylvia stunk. Even if David did sneak down, he had to somehow get Ambrose to ingest the strychnine without leaving any other traces anywhere. In all this, somehow, Ambrose had to ingest it and not notice or spit out the bitter tasting powder. Ambrose would feel the effects in the first 15 to 30 minutes after ingesting the dose. He would have had time to phone 911, call for help or attention. So why did Michael Ambrose die alone, quietly, in his room from such a violent poison? Vomiting, convulsions, pain and even heightened awareness and mania were all commonly associated with strychnine ingestion and toxicity. It was a condition requiring hospitalization and some quick treatment, but it was otherwise survivable unless Ambrose had ingested a massive dose or had been otherwise incapacitated. But there were no straps or restraints in Ambrose's room. His phone was not far away. Why would Michael Ambrose simply die in his bed?

The gravel ended at the driveway's edge as raised beds, made from a couple of 2x4's, formed the boundaries of the parking lot. The cars of each guest sat in their spots. The police had made sure everyone stayed put. The driveway had been blocked off, and officers were posted to the B&B to ensure that the guests didn't leave or sneak off while the investigation continued. Though an arrest had been made, the police were still confirming their facts and wrapping up their case to present before the grand jury.

It occurred to Charlie that the problem he was mulling over was precisely the problem that the police were facing. How did David Elmore poison Michael Ambrose? And of course Elmore, if he was innocent, would have no clue and offer no help. It was a reasonable question, of course, but one that hadn't been satisfactorily answered. If the police gathering evidence didn't have a plausible explanation, and Sylvia or David gave in on the affair, then the entire case would tumble apart like the flimsy straw it was made of.

Charlie took another step and cursed as a sharp pain stabbed into his foot.

"Damnit!" He let out a slight yelp as a stone had lodged itself in his shoe somehow. He huffed in frustration as he knelt and untied his shoe before shaking out and removing the offending piece of driveway gravel. As he began to tie his shoe once more, his eyes fell on a particularly pathetic set of petunias.

Crushed and mangled, so terribly out of place, the delicate flowers were smashed. Charlie frowned and looked to the surrounding area. Nothing else had been disturbed or demolished, but it was very obvious that something had flattened the petunias. The gorgeous purple flowers were ground into the mulch underneath. He looked at the area beyond the petunias. Across the lawn were a set of trash cans. The pristine green grass showed no signs of any wear, and neither did the gravel driveway. Charlie looked back toward the manor and frowned a bit as he thought about the petunias.

Another moment of deliberation more and he stepped over the garden bed and walked onto the lawn, crossing it as he walked toward the garbage cans. He looked over his shoulder again at the grass. As soon as he stepped, the blades began to correct for his steps, and within minutes he couldn't tell where his steps had fallen. Someone had come to these garbage cans that rested back by the padlocked garden shed at the opposite corner of the lawn from the servant's house where the B&B workers stayed. Charlie approached the trio of garbage cans and opened them one at a time. With the amount of trash the business and the employees went through, they needed the extra trash can. The final one was filled with recycling. Glass bottles and metal cans and plastic milk jugs filled the bin. He replaced the lid and opened the second. There were a few trash bags, all neatly tied off to prevent any stench from within. The final one was similar except for one glaring difference. Sitting atop the bags was a glass bottle, thin and tall almost like a wine bottle. The label was face down, so Charlie removed his phone from his pocket and pressed it against the glass lightly to get the bottle to roll over. The label flipped up and Charlie read the yellow lettering on the blue banner background: Campari.

An Italian aperitif bottle was empty, and resting on top of several white trash bags. Charlie frowned and took a picture. Someone had stepped on the petunias and brought something over here. This seemed the most obvious, with the sturdy lock on the garden shed door. There was no freshly turned earth or other suggestion of any other point of interest. Charlie looked over at the first bin, full of recyclables. The glass bottle was certainly misplaced. Perhaps deliberately, or perhaps accidentally. But who would have done that? And when? And why? It was obviously recent since it was resting on top of the trash. The maids hadn't been cleaning since the murder. The police had asked them to refrain for now while the investigation continued.

Charlie swiped on his phone to open the camera function and snapped a picture of the Campari bottle in its place there in the trash can and replaced the lid. He realized a bit too late, of course, that he might have smudged any fingerprints on the trash can lid, and even more to his horror, put his own there. His consolation came from the fact that he'd avoided touching the Campari bottle itself. There might be a dozen fingerprints on the trash can lid, but the glass bottle would have none of his prints on them if anyone checked. For now, he jogged across the lawn and headed back into the B&B, then down the stairs to his room. Once away from any prying eyes, he began to research Campari.

22

Charlie looked at the picture of the Campari bottle on his phone and popped open his laptop, typing in the brand name of the liqueur. Charlie continued his research and furrowed his brow. The door opened and Patience stepped inside, holding a cup of tea.

"I know that look," she said teasingly. "That's the look my husband gets when he's frustrated by a claim and doesn't know how the facts fit together." She walked over to one of the chairs in the room, a comfortably stuffed chair by the gas fireplace and sat down. She sipped her tea and held the mug in both hands. Despite the early summer weather, Patience's slender fingers coiled around the mug for warmth.

"This is the face your husband gets when he feels like he's so close and yet so far, and can't manage to just grab what's in front of him. The face he gets when he solves one problem and two more crop up," he said, punctuating the explanation with a groan.

"What problem?" Patience asked.

Charlie thought for half a moment before answering. Patience was still, technically, a suspect. Though he didn't suspect his own wife for a moment, the police certainly would, so he wondered if by sharing his suspicions if he was truly helping her or just condemning her by giving her information. He decided to risk it. He needed someone to bounce his ideas around with.

"Michael Ambrose was poisoned, killed by strychnine poisoning."

"What does that all mean? I know he's dead, but what does knowing the poison have to do with it? Dead is dead, right?" she asked.

"It matters because of how it was done, dear," Charlie explained, halting as he tried to find the right words. "Ambrose ingested the strychnine. But it has a VERY noticeable and bitter taste to it. It's also a white crystal powder so it's not like he wouldn't have noticed it."

"So the question is, how did someone get him to ingest it without him noticing?" Patience asked.

"Precisely. And more to the point, why would Ambrose be sitting down to eat or drink with David Elmore who threatened to kill him in front of a room full of people? I don't care how long you served together, you need a night or two to pass before you can get over a falling out like that." Charlie frowned and scratched his chin. "Besides, that doesn't explain the taste and texture of the strychnine. I think this whole thing just, completely disproves David's opportunity."

"Opportunity?" Patience asked, furrowing her brow now. "I mean, he could still have done it, right? He lied about where he was at the time of the murder, saying he was in his room when he wasn't."

"He might have lied, but that lie doesn't mean he killed anyone. It just means he can't account for his movements. It's circumstantial. There are a lot of people in Falmouth, Massachusetts who can't tell you where they were or have no witnesses to back them up for their actions that night."

"Then why arrest him?"

"The vial of poison was found in his room, so the police are putting those two facts together and claiming that the killer MUST be Elmore," Charlie said with a shrug.

"So then how DID Ambrose ingest the poison? And if it wasn't David, then who did it?"

"I don't know who did it, but I think I might have found out how it was done."

Patience cocked an eyebrow, remaining silent as she prompted Charlie to continue with a small sip of her tea.

"I found a bottle of alcohol in the trash out back," Charlie explained. "Campari. It's apparently an Italian liqueur, an aperitif."

"Ok. But we're in a really nice B&B honey, isn't it pretty logical that they'd have some alcohol bottles in the trash?"

"Wine, champagne, sure, but this is a specialty liqueur. There's no bar in the B&B. It's something you put into cocktails. Besides that, it wasn't in the recycling. It was in the garbage, just lying on top of the trash bags. If it was thrown out by the staff, it'd be in one of the bags, right?" he suggested.

Patience thought for a moment and nodded as she contemplated it.

"I think someone was drinking with Michael Ambrose the night he was killed. Someone making a drink with Campari. It's very bitter, so it would cover the taste of the strychnine. A few cocktails with someone and Michael would be too drunk to even really notice the symptoms until it was too late, and then he'd likely be too drunk to call for help," Charlie said, a note of fear entering his voice as he spoke. He stood from the bed and walked over to the fireplace to lean against the mantle, fixing Patience with a concerned look. "They've got the wrong man. I'm certain of that, honey. But if I'm right, that means just one thing."

Patience's eyes widened in realization.

The killer was still among them.

23

Charlie and Patience stared at one another when the realization struck both of them.

"What do we do?" Patience asked, a note of panic entering her question.

"Nothing for now. We simply don't know who did it. As long as that person thinks that the police have the killer, there won't be a reason for them to panic. A panicky murderer is the last thing we need."

"But they'll find out soon enough. They already know you're investigating," she pointed out. It was true. They'd all been there to hear Sylvia ask and cajole Charlie into investigating the murder and clearing David's name.

"But they won't know that we've found anything unless someone spills some detail. So this Campari business? Gotta keep that to ourselves. We have to be careful, Patience. This isn't a game or some Agatha Christie novel where the detective always makes it out alive," Charlie said, walking over toward her. He gripped her upper arm firmly and stared into her eyes with concern knit across his face.

Patience stared back, fright evident in the fervent glances as her eyes flickered to and fro, expecting somehow, to catch the murderer listening in on their conversation from the corner of her vision. The whole situation had her upset and overwrought.

"The doors stay locked. You don't accept a drink or food from anyone but me. You don't open the door for anyone unless it's me if you're here alone. Even if it's the police, demand to see a warrant. They can slide it under the door if needs be or show some identification," Charlie told her.

Patience nodded and gripped her husband's arms as if afraid to let him go.

"I'm going to talk to a few other guests. Try to see if I can suss out what happened a bit more, maybe narrow the field of suspects," he said, thumbing over his shoulder to the door.

"Be CAREFUL," she admonished with a serious look.

"I will. But just make sure you don't answer the door unless you know it's me."

Charlie walked over to the door and locked the handle and then waited until he heard his wife click the deadbolt into place. With that assurance in the back of his mind, he ascended the stairs to the main floor. He wanted a cup of tea to help soothe his mind and think a bit.

As he walked into the hall and then the kitchen, he saw the refrigerator door open. It shut after a moment and the figure of Giorgio Scalfani stood with a cup of yogurt in hand. He wore a set of shorts and a simple grey tee shirt, befitting more of a casual athlete than a wealthy financier, however not a spot of sweat seemed to collect on his brow or around his arms.

"Mister Scalfani!" Charlie greeted the Italian gentleman with a friendly wave and a small smile.

"Ah, Signore Callahan!" he returned the greeting with the same formality.

"A little midday snack?" Charlie asked, referring to the yogurt.

Scalfani glanced down at the small yogurt cup in his hand and then smiled at Charlie. "Si, I find myself eating a bit more. This whole affair with the murder." Scalfani said with a bit of a grimace. "It raises the blood pressure and I eat to deal with the stress. Among other things."

"Stress eating isn't healthy, even if you choose healthy snacks. That's what my wife tells me anyway."

"Wives are full of such wisdom," Scalfani replied.

"Don't overeat. Get some exercise. Don't drink too much." Charlie smiled at Scalfani and leaned on the large kitchen island.

"Si. Is all true."

"Mister Scalfani, you came here... Why?" Charlie asked curiously.

"Oh to get away. Enjoy the Cape for a weekend," he replied non-chalantly.

Charlie looked down at his hands on the kitchen island.

"That isn't why."

Scalfani flinched in surprise.

"You came here to talk to Sylvia Montegard. The trial caused the stocks to plummet. Montegard Arms is a key player with other companies in the defense manufacturing sector. And as the world itself edges closer to destabilization, the products they supply to the world are among the most profitable, a profit your accounts can share in thanks to your investments. But the stocks dropping off caused your firm to lose thousands. Hundreds of thousands, perhaps. Please tell me if I'm getting too far off base," Charlie said.

The Italian leaned against the kitchen island and sighed. He set the yogurt cup down and swallowed hard, making the sign of the cross and retrieving a small golden crucifix from inside his shirt to kiss the golden emblem of his faith.

"Millions," he said quietly. "We lost millions of dollars. I was telling my investors, my clients, to ride it out, to let me handle it, but I needed information. I came here hoping to find Sylvia and ask about the company's new projects. New projects could show strength to the market. Cause the stocks to rebound and regain some of their losses."

"And if you had that assurance, you could watch until the losses were recuperated, quietly sell shares, and switch to something a bit more conservative while Montegard Arms went through whatever restructuring they may have to do thanks to this verdict. Get out while the getting's good. A little insider trading and you'd be fine, your clients would be fine, and no one, least of all the SEC, would be any the wiser," Charlie replied.

"God forgive me," Scalfani said quietly. "Please do not think me a bad person, Signore Callahan. I cannot see this business destroyed. I cannot see my family, my clients, destroyed."

"You wanted to save livelihoods, retirements, and your own business after a respected member of an industry and a cornerstone of your investment portfolios crashed hard thanks to a runaway jury that nobody, not even our best analysts, could have foreseen. I don't hold any of that against you, Mister Scalfani."

"And because of this, people might assume I killed Signore Ambrose," Scalfani reasoned.

"Several million dollars is a very good motive for murder. It's certainly been committed for a lot less. Money. Desire. Pride. Anger..." Charlie listed.

"Vanity, Jealousy, and Sloth. Yes. They are called the deadly sins for a reason," Scalfani said. He reached into his pocket and pulled forth a string of black beads, a rosary. Nervously, he ran his fingers over them. "What will you do now with this information?" Scalfani asked.

"Nothing for now, Mister Scalfani. I have no evidence. I have no reason to believe anyone other than David committed the murder," Charlie told him.

"You think Colonel Elmore is guilty? Truly?" he asked.

"I think that David fits all of the facts of the case and lied to police about his whereabouts at the time of the murder," Charlie replied, "And that is all I know at this point."

Scalfani seemed to relax a little at this.

Charlie walked away from the kitchen island, headed over to the pot of hot water on one of the coffee maker burners, and poured himself a cup of steaming hot water. A tea bag selected from the small rack gave him his tea.

"What will you do next then?" Scalfani asked.

"What I've been doing all this time, Mister Scalfani, try to find out who killed Michael Ambrose."

24

Scalfani left the kitchen with his yogurt and headed quietly back to his room after Charlie assured him of his silence. His cup of tea in hand, Charlie walked out onto the veranda that wrapped around the B&B. Sitting in one of the large wicker chairs outside, he sipped his tea and thought. His peace and quiet was disturbed when a second set of footsteps echoed over the wooden beams of the porch floor. The red curly hair bobbing in its tight ringlets announced Angie walking over toward him.

"Hello there!" she chirped like a cheerful little bird. He raised his mug in greeting and sipped the tea. Wearing a set of plush black pajama pants with little pink sheep on them and a matching black tank top, she flopped down into the wicker chair nearby. "So, how goes the detective work?" she asked.

"Detective work?" he asked her curiously.

"Oh, come on. You know, helping to clear the colonel of suspicion of the murder. Catching the real killer, all of that," she said with a coy smirk crossing her features, reaching out to bat playfully at his arm as she sat beside him.

"Well, I don't see that anything's really changed to be honest, but I think the police aren't satisfied. If they were, we'd be back to normal instead of having our chaperones," he said, nodding to the police officer patrolling the front yard keeping an eye on the front portion of the house.

"What do you think they're looking for?" she asked.

"I'm not sure. But I can tell you they've got their work

cut out for them," he replied.

"What do you mean?"

"Michael Ambrose and Colonel Elmore nearly came to blows in the sitting room at the concert. Elmore nearly choked him to death in front of half a dozen people," Charlie explained.

"So? That proves motive doesn't it?"

"Motive for a crime of passion? Yeah. Of course. If Ambrose had been shot or stabbed or even beaten to death, witnesses or no, Elmore would be a wise suspect choice. But poisoning? No. It's too cold, premeditated, and cowardly," Charlie answered.

"Cowardly?! What do you mean? If you're going to take someone's life, that takes a lot more guts than I have," Angie replied with a nervous sort of laugh as she tried to compose herself, seeming a bit flustered at the concept that poisoning was cowardly.

"I mean that Colonel Elmore is a man who has killed people in combat, seen troops under his command wounded or likely even killed, and has maintained his sanity throughout all of it. He's not a man who would shy away from violence as a means to kill. His first and most likely inclination would be to stab, shoot, or strangle Ambrose, or, as we saw, to regain control and fight back against his more violent impulses," he explained, laying out his thoughts for her to follow. "Elmore is the kind of guy who controls his thoughts and keeps himself calm. 'Grace under fire' so to speak, the consummate soldier. So if he were to choose to poison Ambrose, he'd control his violent outbursts. If he did not care to control those outbursts, he'd feel no need to resort to poison him. It's simply contradictory."

"But he lied about his whereabouts and the poison vial

was found in his room."

"Yes, a poison that was ingested. So after the big fight we witnessed, you think these two people who have had such a huge falling out that David literally choked Ambrose in the living room, would sit down and break bread together just a few hours later? Why would he? Both tempers were still running high, both were still quite upset. And on top of all this, I saw Elmore's eyes when he walked into Ambrose's room with me when the maid screamed. He was shocked. Elmore might be a good soldier, but a good actor? I don't think so," Charlie said simply and set down the now empty mug on the boards between his feet, sitting back in the wicker chair to fold his hands over his stomach.

"So you think the police have come to these same conclusions," Angie reasoned.

"I do. I think they're trying to tie up loose ends so this becomes a slam dunk in front of a jury. They can't prove that the strychnine was his, and at a hotel or a B&B, there are people who have access to keys. While Elmore might be lying about where he was last night, they can't even place him here in the B&B at the time of the murder definitively. They can only prove what he wasn't doing: sleeping in his bed. Then comes the coroner's report that shows the poison was ingested, and the police would have to square the ingested poison hours after an assault. A jury would be absolutely right to raise the reasonable doubt that two men would be able to sit down together and share something to drink and eat just hours after one of them threatened to kill the other."

"So you think they've got the wrong man, and you're just a hair away from proving it, aren't you?" Angie taunted a little. Charlie realized a bit more what she was doing, and he cursed himself for being so talkative. Sometimes his job adjusting claims and documenting everything made him run at the mouth a little more than he ever intended.

"I think the police have realized their case is not the slam dunk they thought it was," he said trying his best to be cagey. 'Too little too late,' Charlie thought to himself miserably.

Angie laughed and stood from her chair.

"Oh, I think you've got more than you're going to let on, but I wonder who is going to solve this case faster now, you or Detective Goodwin," she teased as she walked inside.

Charlie sighed and slumped back in the chair a bit as Angie departed.

"Damn," Charlie cursed himself. He'd just finished telling Patience about spilling too much information, and here he was letting someone who could very well be the killer know almost everything he himself did. He only hoped that when Angie mentioned hearing another voice speaking with Michael the night of the murder, she was telling the truth. He certainly believed her when she told him that.

Charlie leaned forward, picked up his empty mug and headed inside toward the kitchen. The dishwasher was the providence of the staff, so the guests were washing their own dishes by hand for a while. He picked up a small sponge and began washing his mug, setting it aside in a dish drainer the staff presumably used for the nicer champagne flutes and wine goblets. Charlie set the mug into the dish drainer, right beside another identical mug, and walked back to his room to speak with Patience.

25

The evening passed as Charlie ordered a pizza for dinner. He and Patience ate quietly in their room downstairs. Charlie ruminated on the information from the day. His conversations with Scalfani and Angie, his conversation with his wife, and the discovery of the Campari bottle all ran through his mind.

"Have you made any progress?" Patience asked after most of the pizza had vanished between them.

"A bit," he said with a slow nod. He was able to commit to that, at least.

"What have you learned, beyond the Campari, that is," she asked him, smiling at her husband as she reached across the last slice of pizza and squeezed his hand.

He managed a smile and squeezed her hand in return and then looked at the last piece of pizza in the box. They generally split things 50/50 like this, but Charlie always seemed to have more of an appetite than his loving wife.

"Go on," she said, rolling her eyes as she withdrew her hand.

Charlie scooped up the final piece and smiled happily before taking a bite.

"I'm convinced that Scalfani is quite probably a consummate liar, or he's just not the murderer," he said.

"What makes you say that?"

"We talked about what he came here for. He was cagey, a bit. But when I pressed him on it and pushed with a supposition I made, he crumbled completely," Charlie answered and looked Patience in the eye. "People lie to me all the time, but their stories are never straight. Their facts are confusing and at odds with reality, and they wind up getting nervous about being discovered in a lie. His lie was so small though, that the lies needed to kill someone, to frame someone else for the murder, and then to lie to police about all of it would be far too much for him."

"What lie did you catch him in?" Patience asked, curious now as she looked over at her husband.

"What amounts as an attempt at insider trading," he replied with a shrug. "I confronted him with the prospect that his business had gone down the tubes, so he did a bit of research on Sylvia, found out that she liked to come up to Falmouth, and followed her up here. He wanted to find out what the company had in store, before the news broke to the press. If he could sell his shares before they truly tanked, he could limit the hemorrhaging of his financial world for himself and his clients and begin working to rebuild all his portfolios. He might be able to keep his clients happy and salvage his business. If she had a few tricks up her sleeve to stage a recovery by strategically announcing certain projects to the press, he could buy up the shares at their current lows and stage an absolute coup. The only killing he'd make would be a financial one on the markets."

"And that was the lie?"

"No, that was the truth, one he felt guilty over. He crossed himself and he asked for forgiveness. He was a man possessed with guilt over being caught."

"Well, what does that prove? Morality for many people is subjective nowadays. He might find murder acceptable, but find theft horrible," Patience said, furrowing her brow. "He could be one of those sociopaths or whatever they are."

"He could be, but, if that were the case, I think he'd be glad to be caught with a little insider trading, especially since I have no evidence to prove it. By giving him an easy explanation for his motives for being here, perhaps a stronger one than killing Michael Ambrose, it stands more to reason that he'd be delighted to have a rationale to give to the police. Prior to our conversation, he just said he was a man who wanted a vacation at the Cape, which is a bit thin given the circumstances. If he told the police my supposition as his actual motive, it's likely that suspicion would move away from him, since he was here to do something unethical and criminal, but never got the chance," Charlie replied. "Besides all of this, the genuine concern he had, the forgiveness he asked for, it wasn't an act. Giorgio Scalfani is a man who goes to confession regularly. I've seen dozens of men like him in line at church for the confessional. He probably still knows all of his prayers in Latin. I can imagine him being an altar server as a boy. He knows right from wrong, and he got caught in the commission of a few sins. The thought of willingly committing a sin was just simply too much and caused the fit of conscience. No, Mister Scalfani is precisely who he says he is. He didn't want to be here in the first place. I'd lay odds on it."

"I'm not so sure how you can be so certain," Patience said and sighed as she stood, letting her hair down from the bun she'd put it in. She shook out her curls and headed over toward the bathroom. She began her evening ritual of preparing for bed as Charlie took care of the empty pizza box, setting it outside the door in the trash bin provided by the police. Shutting the doors and locking them securely, he made sure the shades were drawn as well. He began his own nightly routine.

Patience finished her evening routine and let Charlie

have the bathroom as she returned to the room in a white silk nightgown. Charlie wasn't far behind, having far less to take care of before he joined her.

As they shared the bed, Charlie wrapped an arm around Patience's slender frame and he pressed a kiss to her shoulder.

"I worry about you, Charlie," she said in the darkness as the married couple enjoyed some peace and quiet.

"I worry about me too, dear, but we shouldn't worry about tomorrow until tomorrow. We're safe for now. We've got each other. We'll see what new worries tomorrow brings," Charlie said. Once more, his lips pressed to his wife's shoulder, and he closed his eyes to sleep.

26

The night passed fitfully. Charlie didn't sleep well and did his best to keep his tossing and turning to a minimum. When he woke the next morning, he got up and staggered into the bathroom, pouring himself a glass of water to wash the taste of morning breath out of his mouth briefly. He stared at himself in the mirror. He'd seen every line, every grey hair in his mustache and beard, every wrinkle and blemish a thousand times over, but before recently there was nothing there that surprised him or caused him to feel dissociation from the face in the mirror. Today it was like getting a glimpse into a world of 'may have beens'. Charlie was safe. Charlie didn't take risks. Risks were terrible things. He hated them. The insureds went into risk pools. They shared their money to mitigate the costs of the risks that didn't pan out. These were simple straightforward risks. These were small risks like gunning it through that light that was yellow and turning red, turning left from a stop sign onto a main road, driving five or ten miles over the speed limit because you were late to work. But, of course, they were managed risks more or less. Every day these things happened thousands, if not millions of times. And how many of them resulted in accidents? And of those how many resulted in injuries? Deaths? Perhaps less than a tenth of a percent of the number of little managed risks resulted in something bad. His life was spent cleaning up those risks. His career, his job, his skillset, designed to investigate those risks and to one extent or another, wipe away the consequences of those risks that had gone wrong with the great equalizer: money.

He didn't take risks. Charles Francis Callahan was the man who settled risks, who told people to drive safely, who would turn right at the stop sign and make a U-turn on a green arrow later instead of turning left. And yet the man who stared into his eyes in the mirror was hunting a murderer. He was putting his life, and the life of his wife, on the line to hunt down someone who, in cold blood, poisoned a man leaving him to die in excruciating agony. This man who stared into Charlie's eyes was a risk-taker. He was a hunter, a man who pursued, for reasons unknown, a sense of justice. The police were looking for quick and expedient answers to the obvious questions. They had means, motive, and opportunity and their investigation was ready to be put to bed. But this creature hungered for something more. Why?

Charlie simply had no answers. He stood up straight and took a deep breath before he turned to the shower and began his morning preparations. As he was coming out, Patience sat awake in the bed, hair askew and looking somewhat like a boiled owl. If ever there was a face that expressed a need for coffee, it was that one.

He walked over toward the travel bag and withdrew some clothes. A tee shirt and a set of jeans would suffice for the day, he decided. Perhaps a light sweatshirt would be fine. He waited for his wife to finish up her rather quick morning routine. She threw her hair into a messy bun after a quick morning wash up and the two of them headed upstairs. Breakfast was brought out. A waffle, some fresh fruit, and coffee comprised a nice morning meal. No one spoke as they sat down and ate. The only sound was the echoing of flatware on plates as everyone ate in silence. Charlie took the opportunity to review his phone. Tweets about local news flashed across his screen. One caught his eye.

Calvin Hodges, a news aggregator and part time opinion columnist had a flashy new headline that he reposted that day.

DO POLICE HAVE THE WRONG MAN IN THE AMBROSE MURDER CASE?

Charlie stared at the headline. His eyes could have fallen from their sockets in pure shock! He clicked the article link and followed it through.

The opinion piece, picked up by several major news outlets, went into detail. Hodges started out by supposing that Elmore was the killer, and laid out a compelling case as to why he was being arrested, but then changed direction. A career military man resorting to poison? A violent conflict followed by that poison being ingested mere hours after threats of harm and death? As Hodges unwound the case, one strand at a time, the reader naturally came to the conclusion Hodges intended them to: that Colonel Elmore was simply the least likely suspect, though Hodges did concede that lying to the police apparently over his alibi for the murder was a true and very serious problem to overcome.

After laying out the arguments that Charlie was all too familiar with, the article proceeded to arrive at the conclusion that the police had failed in their duty to actually catch the murderer, and with the investigation ongoing, Hodges suggested that the police knew this as well as he did. The threat Hodges wrote at the end was almost exactly what he and Patience had discussed. If Elmore was the wrong man, that meant that a murderer still stalked the stairs and rooms of The Safe Harbor B&B.

Charlie read the article twice more.

The breakfast dishes were cleared away by the staff who

went about washing them and cleaning up.

Guests left the dining area and dispersed.

Charlie caught a look at one in particular. The bobbing red curls of Angie Harris bounced along as she walked into the living room, the room where the whole confrontation occurred. She had a brilliant smile on her face that morning, almost looking like the proverbial cat that ate a canary for breakfast instead of a waffle and fruit. She sat down in one of the large sitting chairs before the fireplace and pulled out her phone.

Charlie followed her into the room, telling Patience to go back to their room and he would be with her in a moment.

"So who is Calvin Hodges to you? Your boyfriend? A cousin? Step sibling or something? Good friend?" he asked, searching for some recognition as he named off the relations and crossed his arms over his chest.

"Who?" She asked in return.

"You know damn well who. You and I talked just yesterday and now suddenly everything I say to you is printed in the Boston, Providence, and Hartford news!" he snapped at her.

Angie's smile disappeared into a wicked scowl.

"I don't know what you're talking about," she said, crossing her arms.

"You do," Charlie said and sighed heavily, "and I can't believe you're treating this so flippantly!"

"What? No one can make the connection. It's just some random blogger making a comment about the case, making some observations."

"Observations that they wouldn't be making unless they were right here, unless they knew details about this that aren't public knowledge. Observations that will point directly back to someone in this B&B. Everything in that article came from our conversation, and I can vouch for myself and my wife, but not for you."

"Fine. I'll take the article down and ask for a retraction from the papers. You happy?"

"You?!?" Charlie asked, his eyes going wide as he stood straight.

"Yes, me," Angie hissed. "You don't understand, journalism is still a man's world out there. They take people like me, and throw us puff pieces, and leave the best stories and leads to the men. A man is hard hitting, a woman is bitchy. A man is incisive, a woman is biting. A man is astute, a woman is nitpicky. The double standards are alive and well in journalism, so I created Calvin to publish stuff that would otherwise get ignored if it came from Angela Harris."

Charlie listened as she spoke. Tears began to well in her eyes.

"You have to retract those stories, Angie, and I recommend you keep yourself locked in your room until this is all sorted out."

"Why? Why should I be a prisoner-" she began.

"Because, those suppositions are correct! The police have the wrong man and they know it, but they haven't squared David Elmore away. Was he working with someone? Was he not working with someone? He has means, motive, and opportunity, but it's all weak. They can't put it all together, and if one person comes forward to substantiate where David was, that's it. The opportunity is gone and the cops are back looking for everyone else. But if the killer thinks he or she isn't safe? Then none of us are safe, especially if they think we're on their trail."

Angie was silent for several moments.

"And what makes you think I'm not the killer?" she asked.

Charlie sighed and leaned against the mantle.

"If you were, you would be glad to see the cops chasing someone else down and charging them with the crime. The criminal always wants to get away with it unless they're out to get caught. And this isn't a case where someone wants to get caught. Whoever killed Michael Ambrose wanted to get away with it."

Angie grew silent and stood after a few moments.

"And you telling me this means you think I'm not the one who killed Michael Ambrose," she concluded.

"I already said I don't. I don't think you have a real motive for wanting to kill him, and I don't think you'd go through all the trouble of planning out and poisoning him, plus as I said, if you were the killer, you wouldn't be trying to shift blame off of Elmore," Charlie reasoned.

Angie nodded quietly, listening to his rationale.

"I think I'm going to take your advice, Mister Callahan," she announced quietly.

Charlie breathed a sigh of relief.

"Thank God!"

Angie walked out of the sitting room quietly and headed back toward her room. Charlie stood in the sitting room and looked at the fireplace, quietly thinking of his next move. The field of suspects was growing ever narrower, but if he was going to pursue Ambrose's killer, he needed more information. He walked away from the hearth and headed back to his room. It was time to reopen the insurance claim file.

27

Charlie sighed as Patience tried to distract herself with a set of knitting needles and a skein of bright green yarn. The laptop open in front of Charlie displayed names and file notes, payments to attorneys, and expert reports. This was where it all began, Charlie felt sure of that. Michael Ambrose's murder was not the beginning of a story, it was the culmination of a story whose climax was much earlier: the trial. If not for the verdict, would Michael have been murdered? If Elmore was the killer, it was quite possible. Even if the civil suit had turned out as a defense verdict, Michael's accusations and role as a star for the plaintiff attorneys made him an enemy of Elmore's for life. The accusations, uncertainty, and rumors would always follow Elmore unless Michael was dead.

And yet, Michael was dead, and Elmore was the prime suspect. He simply fit the mold too well for the police to ignore. He wanted Ambrose dead. His entire livelihood with his promising military career as a highly decorated officer was at an end because Ambrose let loose a dirty little secret. In perhaps another decade of service, the name Elmore would be spoken of in the same breath as Mattis, Powell, Schwarzkopf, MacArthur, and Bradley. That alone was more than enough reason to kill a lowly first lieutenant who made a lifelong career out of being a professional pain in the rear. The question that dogged Charlie and made him second guess himself, however, was the same question that dogged the police even now.

What had Elmore been doing the night of the murder?

The police didn't know. They only knew he hadn't been in his bed and that the poison was found there. Where he was, nobody on the force could say. That was where Charlie had a slight edge. He'd spoken to Sylvia. He'd watched the two interact throughout the claim cycle. He'd been there at both of their depositions and throughout every single day of the trial. He watched them sit near one another, speaking quietly in a hallway when they thought nobody would notice. There was more there. The question that nipped at the back of Charlie's mind, was whether or not the 'more' was love.

He was almost certain that David and Sylvia were carrying on an affair. He was also certain that Sylvia stood to lose just as much, if not more, than David. Her family fortune, her company, her entire future as an independent heiress and force in the military industrial complex was at stake. While Elmore might have become a general, Montegard Arms collapsing from this suit could mean the end of generations of arms manufacturing history and destruction of an empire. Was David Elmore worth all of that? And why didn't she come forward to confess quietly that there was an affair? Surely her husband, while he would make out like a bandit, would otherwise be mollified by some decent settlement from Sylvia's attorneys. A good fixer, a signed document and no contest in the divorce and the whole affair would be quietly buried while her husband went off to enjoy the life of a playboy with 6 or 7 figures worth of Sylvia's money in a nice trust account for him. The affair simply wasn't the biggest risk for someone like her who could afford the very best, and yet, here she was keeping secrets. The affair was being kept quiet, and only by bullying his way into her privacy had he discovered the truth.

Even that was a question. Had he discovered the real truth? Or just what Sylvia wanted him to believe?

Charlie rubbed his temples in frustration.

"You're back at square one again, aren't you?" Patience asked with a studious glance crossing her features.

"I'm just wondering," he started and trailed off.

"Wondering what?"

He didn't speak for several moments.

"What if Elmore was set up?" he posed the question to her. Patience blinked in surprise.

"Who would want to?" she asked.

"The murderer. Elmore's outburst is perfect. He swore in front of half a dozen people he wanted to kill Ambrose, and the next morning Michael Ambrose winds up dead from a horrible alkaline poisoning."

"The murderer is on good terms with Elmore. Hypothetically, they drug him with a simple sleeping pill, perhaps something as simple as a few crushed nighttime sleep aids. Over the counter garbage. He's out. They steal the key to his room while he's unconscious. They kill Ambrose. They plant the evidence in Elmore's room. Then they put the key back and Elmore eventually wakes up in time to discover Ambrose's body the next morning. Elmore dashes right there into the doorway in time to actually be surprised to see his former first lieutenant dead." Charlie laid out the story that formed in his mind, step by step.

Patience listened.

"He would be surprised, then. He'd be truly surprised to see Ambrose dead. And he wouldn't have any explanation for the poison bottle found in his room or where he was the previous night," Patience explained.

"But he did," Charlie said, responding to her.

"But his explanation was a lie. He said he was in his room, but the bed had never been slept in," she pointed out.

"His explanation might be the only one he knew. If he was drugged, he might have been completely out of it. He might know he was in *a* bed and just assumed it was HIS bed. Elmore might be lying unintentionally."

"But then if someone did drug him, he would have had contact with someone prior to falling asleep, he would tell the police, and they could follow the same trail of thought that you are," Patience reasoned.

Charlie frowned and clutched his chin in his hand as he leaned on the small table that functioned as his desk with his laptop propped open.

"Unless he was trying to hide that person's identity."

Patience looked as though she'd been slapped by that statement. Her eyes widened.

"You think he met someone, the murderer, for some sort of rendezvous, and they drugged Elmore and killed Ambrose?"

"I think," Charlie began, "that murder is a very messy and serious business that doesn't fit into convenient little boxes. There are plots within plots. Riddles within riddles. I think I need to speak with Detective Goodwin."

Patience let out a sigh and looked at her husband, cocking her head to the side.

"But you don't believe this new theory, this new idea, do you?" she asked pointedly.

It was Charlie's turn to look like he had been smacked.

"What do you mean?" he asked.

"I mean just what I said. I know you, Charles Francis Callahan. Do you remember when we first got married and you were working under that awful manager at Great Alliance Mutual? The one that made you doubt yourself that you were even a decent insurance adjuster?" she pointed out.

"Ugh, how could I forget?" he winced.

"You second guessed every decision. You second guessed yourself. You refused to commit to anything without talking to your supervisor first about all of it. You accepted only one thing as a fact: that you were a bad adjuster and didn't know what you were doing."

Charlie hung his head a bit shamefully.

"But you weren't a bad adjuster. You were just a desk adjuster with a micro-manager who didn't know what they were talking about. They second guessed you at every turn to make themselves feel better, like they were 'coaching' and 'developing' you. If they graded you based on how you actually performed, they would have realized you didn't need coaching and development. Then you left the company. You moved on and began doing great things. You started out slowly, but soon you moved up. You had one promotion after another, and then wound up being - THE major case handler for your entire company. Everyone from your direct manager to the vice presidents of the company trust you. Charlie, we ate at the CEO's house last Christmas at his private dinner party! You know what you're doing Charlie. And I can see right now you're second guessing yourself. Whatever this is, you don't believe it yourself," she said.

Charlie was silent for several long moments.

"You're right."

Patience quieted down and looked at him, almost unsure.

"You're right," he repeated quietly. "I'm second guessing myself."

She nodded a little.

"Sometimes that's healthy, but I don't think your instincts are wrong, honey. You're doing something here that is putting your skills to use."

"Maybe. I think I need to talk to Detective Goodwin." Charlie rose and shut his laptop. Reviewing the claim file hadn't yielded anything further, but now he felt at least good enough about his conclusions to cast serious doubt on the detective's conjecture that David was the murderer. He walked outside and spoke to the officer, asking him to get word to Detective Goodwin for him, and walked back into his room.

28

Martin Goodwin had grown up in Boston. The son of two cops who soon after his birth became two divorced cops, he found that he liked quiet and hated the stress of conflict. He liked the peace of the small New England villages and towns, so when he went to college for a criminal justice degree and passed the police academy, he did his best to find assignments in small towns. Promotions came up, and he would apply, moving from town to town, from village to village across the quiet countryside. Murder was uncommon. Burglaries and criminal mischief were usually all he had to deal with. Somehow, in Goodwin's experience, New Englanders were just too polite for the messy business of murder. It caused too much commotion for the descendants of quiet gentlemen farmers. This was the way Goodwin preferred it to be. It was a lot less money than he'd make in a bigger department in Boston, or Providence, or Hartford, but it was a lot less work and quieter work. Instead of investigating gang slayings, drug overdoses, and randomly found bodies that nobody could identify or knew anything about, his case load was quieter.

Detective Goodwin stepped out of his car and looked at the thorn in his side, The Safe Harbor Bed and Breakfast. Falmouth was full of little tourist serving businesses. From boutique restaurants to bed and breakfasts to little museums and antique shops, the town of Falmouth was built for quiet tourists, the kind who loved the sea and quiet little afternoons eating good seafood and watching the surf. The

Safe Harbor was one of the nicest establishments in town and had a reputation for being quiet and centrally located.

He walked toward the main entrance and climbed the stairs, jogging up the white wooden steps to the front door. One of the persons of interest involved, Charles Callahan, had put through a message, asking the detective to drop by. He had further information. Goodwin grunted as he opened the door and stepped into the main hallway, the hardwood floor echoing under the black dress shoes he wore as each step brought him along further into the B&B.

"Detective!" Charlie called. He stood by the check in desk, a small alcove that had been built into the hallway with a laptop and cash box. Charlie walked toward the detective, and Goodwin shook his hand.

"Mister Callahan," Martin said with a sharp nod and a firm shake.

*   *   *

Charlie waited patiently for Detective Goodwin to show up. He waited in the sitting room, quietly pacing about as he sipped a bottle of water. The waiting was making him a bit nervous. What exactly was he going to tell Goodwin that he didn't already know? Was he going to put forward pure conjecture and invite more scrutiny onto Sylvia? Was he going to bring that scrutiny down on her and Elmore by revealing what he knew about their affair? Callahan still had no clue what he would tell Goodwin. When the car door slammed and Charlie saw Detective Goodwin head toward the front entrance, he left the sitting room to meet him by the desk. Charlie walked over and stood there as the door opened. The detective seemed somehow irritable, as if nothing was going his way that day.

As they shook hands, Charlie felt a small pang of guilt at bringing him out here.

"Mister Callahan," Martin said with a sharp nod and a firm shake.

"I'm glad you could make it on such short notice, Detective. I think I may have some further information to help your investigation."

"Oh? And you didn't bring this to my attention before because...?" Goodwin asked searchingly, peering at Charlie.

"I only just found out myself. Let's go into the sitting room for a bit more privacy and talk," Charlie said quietly.

"If we must," the detective said with a sigh. The two men walked toward the sitting room and took seats in the two high backed chairs by the fireplace.

"So, do you want to tell me what this is all about Mister Callahan?" Goodwin asked.

"Elmore isn't your man," Charlie said confidently.

"Oh? And tell me why not? His entire career was derailed by Ambrose's reports and the trial. Did you know he was a hair's breadth from a court martial? He was given a quiet back room alternative: he could have everything exposed and risk being drummed out or retire immediately and get a discharge to avoid scandal and exposure. Covering up the flawed M87 replacement from Montegard Arms would have brought not only scandal on him, but on the entire US Armed Forces. They were in collateral damage mode, and as far as they were concerned, Elmore caused it. Ambrose killed his career, showed up and made a perfect ass of him yet again in a social setting. Ambrose seemed to dog his heels. Elmore even swore in front of witnesses that he would kill him. You are one of those witnesses, Mister

Callahan. The next morning Ambrose is dead, Elmore has no alibi, the vial of poison is in Elmore's room, and Elmore lies about having slept there. So tell me, Mister Callahan, why is this not an open and shut case of a revenge killing?" Goodwin laid out the whole case and frowned at Charlie.

Charlie sighed a bit and looked at Goodwin. He could tell the detective thought this was all a colossal waste of time, but he nodded to each one of Goodwin's points.

"You're certainly correct about all that. Elmore has a motive. Elmore said he'd kill Ambrose. Elmore lied about where he was the night of the murder. The poison was found in Elmore's room. But you haven't charged him with the murder, and you haven't closed the case to put it before a grand jury, which tells me even as certain as you are that you've got the right suspect, you still have doubts," Charlie ventured and nodded to Detective Goodwin.

The red-headed man frowned.

"Elmore swore he would kill Ambrose and nearly choked the life out of him. It took two of us to pull him off the man. They hated each other. They were men of violence. Ambrose had never seen combat, but Elmore had. He was a man comfortable with killing the enemy, possibly even in close contact," Charlie said. "And what's more, while the poison bottle was found in Elmore's room, you know as well as I do that what matters is what the poison was. It was ingested, wasn't it? Strychnine, an alkaloid poison."

Goodwin frowned and grunted a little bit.

"It tastes bitter, and it was ingested. So how did he ingest it? Within hours of nearly being choked to death, having a violent confrontation with his former commanding officer, Ambrose sits down and has a snack or a drink with the same man that tried to kill him? No. Please. You don't believe that and neither do I, and you know a jury wouldn't believe it either," Charlie asserted.

"You make a good point," Goodwin cautiously agreed. 'But however it happened, we have no alibi for him and the poison in his room. It's a leap, I grant you, but we can place him there with means, motive, and opportunity, so I'm not sure what you want to try to prove."

"And what if he had a reason to lie? A reason to protect someone?" Charlie suggested.

"Are you suggesting Elmore is protecting the murderer?" Martin asked.

"I'm suggesting that David may have a completely unrelated reason to lie about where he was that night."

"A reason more serious than facing life in prison for murder?" Martin asked, an eyebrow arching curiously.

"If he knows he didn't do it and thinks he can beat the wrap, sure, he loses nothing but time. He gets an acquittal with a good lawyer and you lose your primary murder suspect. His secret is safe. The real murderer gets away. You are literally the only one who loses out in this scenario," Charlie said, laying out the case.

Martin frowned and let out a huff of frustration.

"All right, let's say I believe you, and I'm not saying I do, hypothetically, where would Elmore have been if he wasn't in his bed the night Ambrose was killed?" Martin asked, leaning back and folding his hands, studying Charlie with a searching gaze.

"Someone else's."

Martin blinked in surprise as if he'd been punched. The red-headed detective's eyes flashed with insight.

"But why would he hide that? He's not a married man. This is the 21st century!" Martin spat, frowning as he rejected the idea.

"Because his lover wants the affair kept a secret. A secret that Elmore, being the man he is, will keep even if it means taking risks by facing a murder charge. And remember, once acquitted, he can no longer be tried a second time. Even if more information comes forward," Charlie replied.

"Yeah, double jeopardy, I'm well aware," Martin said, and waved dismissively. But even as he voiced the objection and listened to Charlie's answer, Charlie saw the doubt winning out in his mind.

"Who?" Martin asked.

"I've been asked to keep that confidential, but I can confirm that's what Elmore was up to. If you ask him, telling him you don't care who, you don't know who, he might even confirm it. He might even give you the name if you keep his alibi out of the papers," Charlie replied. He looked up suddenly as a number of thumping noises echoed from the back staircase. Martin gave him a curious look.

"This means we're back to the beginning with -" Martin began, and was cut off with a startled shriek that destroyed the peace of the B&B.

Charlie and Martin jolted up and nearly collided as they stood from the seats. Both men made their way toward the back staircase. There at the base of the stairs was a woman's form, red hair matted with blood. A few stairs above her lay a bronze statue of a cat.

Patience stood in shock over the body of Angie Harris.

29

Patience stared in shock at Charlie and then her gaze flicked over to Detective Goodwin. Her arms trembled and she twitched as she stood there. Charlie took a step forward just as his wife lost consciousness, fainting away, and reached out to catch her. Charlie scooped her up in his arms.

"A second murder," Goodwin murmured as he stood over the body of the young journalist.

Charlie gently cradled his wife and stroked her cheek, holding her to keep her breathing smoothly. He gently tapped her cheek to try to bring her around.

"And your primary suspect is still in a holding cell, locked up and under guard," Charlie replied with a harsh whisper. He frowned and looked down at Angie with a forlorn sigh. Patience moaned in his arms and her eyes fluttered open. She turned her head and looked toward Angie and gasped, sitting bolt upright.

Her head smacked into Charlie's jaw and he lost his grip, dumping Patience unceremoniously to the floor with a grunt of pain from both of them.

Charlie rubbed his jaw and Patience stood, scrambling away and using the bannister to pull herself up to her feet.

"So, do you want to tell me how this happened Mrs. Callahan?" Goodwin asked.

"My wife had nothing to do with this!" Charlie exclaimed, completely flabbergasted at the mere suggestion that Patience might be responsible.

"I asked her the question, not you," Goodwin said

pointedly. Charlie frowned and silenced himself. Patience shuddered.

"I was in our room. I came up to get a cup of tea in the kitchen, just something to drink, and when I was making the tea, I heard several thumping noises. I came out here to see what the noises were, and..." Patience trailed off, staring at the limp body.

The uniformed officers were locking down the place and one was radioing to their dispatch to send out a team to collect whatever evidence could be collected. The coroner, of course, was apprised and dispatched.

A small digital trill of notes echoed from the kitchen.

"What's that?" Goodwin asked.

"My tea," Patience answered with a far-away look in her eyes. "Oh, Charlie, I want to go home." She whimpered and turned to her husband. Charlie embraced her and held her tightly in his arms.

Goodwin got up and walked into the kitchen. He returned moments later, looking at Patience.

"Your tea is finished," Goodwin said.

Patience didn't respond.

"You say when you heard the thumps, you came out here to see what the noise was?" he asked.

"Y-yes," she replied.

"Did you see anyone? Or hear anyone running away?" Goodwin asked.

"N-no," she answered between sobs.

"What's going-" Sylvia Montegard began at the top of the stairs, followed by a sharp gasp. She wore a set of white capris and a navy blue blouse with a golden anchor motif embroidered around the midsection.

Charlie and Goodwin looked up at the woman.

A door opened and was followed by a hearty yawn from upstairs. Sylvia turned to see who it was.

Edward Whitehall walked out, wearing a simple white tee and some boxers while he tied his terry cloth robe around his waist.

"Can't someone take an afternoon nap in peace without-" he began, shock registering on his face at the scene below.

Another door opened and shut and Mister Scalfani appeared at Edward's shoulder. The commotion of Sylvia's question and Edward's reaction apparently drew him out.

"Holy Mary, Mother of God!" Scalfani swore and crossed himself as he saw the body at the foot of the stairs.

Sylvia stepped imperiously down the stairs and frowned.

"What happened here?" she demanded as she walked over toward Charlie holding on to Patience.

"Patience found Miss Harris as you see her now. Someone killed her, Mrs. Montegard," Goodwin responded. Charlie nodded in confirmation.

"Someone? You mean someone other than David," she asserted.

"It would be rather difficult to blame David for this since he's miles away in a cell under guard," Charlie said dryly.

Goodwin scowled at Charlie as he said that.

Sylvia turned to Patience and gently rubbed a hand over her back.

"Your poor wife. Is there anything I can do?" she asked sympathetically.

"I think maybe it would be best if she goes back to our room to lie down," Charlie said and looked at Patience. She let out a small whimper and nodded.

"I haven't finished my questions, Mister Callahan," Goodwin warned.

"Look at the body, Detective. Angie was hit so hard it caved in the back of her skull and likely spattered blood onto the hands and arms of the person who killed her. But my wife's hands are completely clean. Not a speck of blood on her clothes, either!" Charlie replied in an exasperated tone. "There is no way Patience committed this murder. The evidence doesn't back it up and Patience's story matches to the tea going off in the kitchen."

Goodwin scowled at Charlie.

"I don't want to have to remind you, Mister Callahan, that YOU are a person of interest in this entire affair, and that I am the detective!" he snapped.

Charlie frowned in return.

"Well, since you arrested the wrong man for the murder, and now a second murder confirms that you've got the wrong person in custody, I'd think you were interested in a little help from someone who investigates accidents, arson, and other little problems for a living," Charlie responded coldly.

Goodwin narrowed his gaze, but huffed and turned away, ordering an officer to accompany Patience back to her room.

"While this is investigated, your wife will be kept safe and remain under police guard," Goodwin said. Patience and the Officer walked down the stairs into the basement room that was occupied by Charlie and Patience.

Goodwin took his phone out and snapped a few photos while they waited for a coroner.

Sylvia stood at Charlie's side.

"Why didn't we hear anything other than the thumps?"

she asked.

"What do you mean?" Charlie asked, turning his head to look at her.

"I mean, why didn't Miss Harris cry out? No screams. No shouts of anger. No nothing," she explained.

"Whoever it was killed her in one, hard, perfect blow. Death was probably instantaneous. Angie never had time to cry out. Probably didn't even know her killer was following her. No shouts. No screams. Just poor Miss Harris being killed," Charlie explained and looked down at the body once more.

"She was so young," she said softly.

"She was. Poor kid. I told her to stay as safe as she could," Charlie said.

"Was she in danger?" Sylvia asked curiously.

"She knew some things about the murder. Things she wasn't telling people, but things she otherwise let slip very publicly. It made her a possible target," Charlie said with a little sigh.

Sylvia's eyes widened a bit.

"You asked me to investigate, so I have been," Charlie told her as he caught the surprise in her gaze. "Everyone knows something about what happened. Everyone knows a little about the murder."

"Everyone has a connection," Sylvia said quietly.

"Connection..." Charlie said, his voice trailing off. He blinked in surprise as his eyes widened and without another word, dashed back down to his room.

"That's it!" he cried as he clattered down the stairs.

30

Charlie flew downstairs toward his room and nearly ran face first into the chest of the officer standing outside his door. He skidded to a stop and avoided falling over as he reached for the door handle.

"Sorry, sir, but nobody is allowed in or out," the officer said.

"What!? This is ridiculous, this is my room. I'm here with my wife, Patience!" Charlie exclaimed incredulously.

"I don't care, sir, I'm charged with guarding the woman inside and making sure she doesn't leave and nobody goes in. She may have seen something or heard something more than what she said, and someone might be trying to kill her, too. That's what Detective Goodwin said," the officer said firmly.

"Look, Officer. I just need to get in there to get my laptop," he replied.

The officer looked at him warily.

"You can come in with me and watch me get my laptop. I promise I won't try anything, and I certainly won't hurt my own wife. You can even ask her to get my laptop for me! I'll wait right here," Charlie pled.

The officer frowned, but turned and knocked at the door.

"Miss?" he called through the door.

The door opened a moment later and Patience stood there, eyes stained with tears.

"Charlie!" she said, her voice torn with anguish as she tried to get close to him, needing the comfort only her husband could give her.

Charlie took two steps forward before the officer intercepted them.

Patience let out a little wail of sadness.

"Patience, honey, I might be able to get all this cleared up. I need my laptop sweetheart," Charlie said. Patience sniffled and nodded, turning back to the room. A few moments passed and she handed over the computer. The officer gave it an appraising look before nodding and taking it to hand over to Charlie.

"Thanks," Charlie muttered to the officer. "I'll get this all sorted as quickly as I can, honey. I promise!"

Patience cried and turned back into the room. The officer shut the door behind her.

Charlie frowned at the officer.

"My wife's heart is breaking and she's been through the most traumatic experience she's likely ever faced in her life and likely ever will face," Charlie said. "All she wants is the comfort of her husband to help her through this."

"And I have my orders," the officer replied, dispassionately.

Charlie huffed and turned to stalk back up the stairs. His own heart was breaking, but instead of tears of anguish and sorrow, he was enraged that he couldn't be there to comfort his wife. Patience was a gem among women and the shining treasure in his life. To see her in this state and have someone stand between them was maddening.

He stalked into the living room and sat down at the small dining table area, opening the laptop and connecting to his claim system remotely. He typed his login information into the query box and blinked in surprise. Access Denied. What? Charlie was on leave, but his access shouldn't be denied outright! He was still an employee in good standing

His reviews wouldn't be happening until after the trip was over. He tried again. Access Denied. Once more. "Access Denied" and "Account Locked" flashed on the screen. A small tooltip told him to contact his system administrator if he had further issues.

He frowned and went back to the login screen. His account was denied access and locked. He hated having to do this, but there was no alternative. At his company he occasionally had to back up his counterparts while they were out of the office. They backed him up while he was on vacation as well. The industry was good like that on the whole, always having a backup and assigning people to support one another.

He tapped 'thawthorne' into the username box. Ten little asterisks appeared in the password box as he used his backup's login. Tim had a few sensitive files that were locked down to only him, and he'd given Charlie his login information a week or two after the trial ended. It wasn't something they were supposed to do, but those sensitive files needed to be handled while he was gone to his mother's funeral in Idaho. The computer communicated with the network and his desktop, or rather, Tim's desktop, opened up.

He clicked his way into the claim system and began typing in the claim number. There was a connection here that he wasn't seeing, there was something that had escaped his notice. Everyone had a connection to Michael Ambrose. Everyone was here for one reason or another.

He pulled up the claim file and began scrolling through the documents. Payments had been issued to dozens of attorneys representing the estates, and he clicked through each estate document, searching one after the other until he found what he was looking for.

After getting through half of them, he found it. On the 7th document, there on the line labeled 'Executor/Executrix', he read a name, and cursed softly.

"That's the connection," he whispered. He saved the document and sent it to himself in an email, his private email. He'd catch hell for all this later, but he'd explain everything in time.

He logged out and shut down the laptop, looking at his phone now as it displayed '1 New Email' on the screen.

*   *   *

The coroner came quickly enough and confirmed what was evident. Angie Harris had been killed by a blow to the back of the head with what was likely the cat statue as a murder weapon. Some small white fibers were stuck in the wound, and there was a curious lack of blood on the statue itself for something that had landed so heavily in the redhead's skull.

Goodwin and the coroner were talking quietly as the body was lifted onto the gurney and covered before being wheeled out the front door. The bronze statue of the cat was bagged and tagged for evidence. Two officers were even removing the carpet from the stairs, ripping it up to take in to evidence.

Charlie stood back, phone in hand as he waited to speak with Goodwin.

The detective waved him over.

"- about halfway down the stairs," the coroner said. His black hair was tied in tight cornrows, neatly kept. He wore a set of slacks and a sport coat over a blue dress shirt. A small notepad and pen were in his hand as he made his initial observations and shared them with Goodwin.

"Mister Callahan," Goodwin said in acknowledgment with a nod of his head.

"Ahhh, so it was your wife who discovered the body," the coroner said, nodding to Charlie, gesturing toward him with his pen.

"Yes. Charlie Callahan," he said, and stuck out a hand to shake.

"Doctor Jean Louvois," the coroner said, shaking Charlie's hand firmly.

"Thank you, Jean," Goodwin said with a nod. "I'll talk to you back at the station and we'll discuss everything there."

Doctor Louvois nodded and turned to follow the body out to the coroner's van.

"Is there something further, Mister Callahan?" Goodwin asked, his voice holding an edge of confrontation. He was getting rather tired of dealing with the fussy little insurance man.

Charlie frowned a little, hiding his embarrassment.

"So she was struck halfway down the stairs and tumbled the rest of the way?" Charlie asked, pointing to the officers still working on tearing up the stair runner rug.

"Yes. Whoever hit her probably followed her down the stairs, hit her over the head with the bronze statuette, and then fled from there," Goodwin surmised.

"Up the stairs," Charlie supplied.

"What?" Goodwin asked.

"They had to go up the stairs," Charlie expounded.

Goodwin looked at the scene and then back to Charlie a bit shrewdly.

"And how did you reach this deduction?" he asked curiously.

"If they'd run down the stairs, where would they go?

Martin, they would run into one of your officers at any exit, Patience in the kitchen, or us in the living room. The only places they could go would be our room, which was locked in the basement, and Michael Ambrose's room which is also locked. They simply had to go back up the stairs," Charlie reasoned and pointed out. Goodwin thought for a moment and nodded. It was a sound conclusion.

"Unless they were already in the hall past us. We went out the back door of the living room toward the back stairs. They could have been down the hall behind us," Goodwin pointed out.

"But they still wouldn't have had anywhere to go. They would have been trapped simply by the officers outside. They would have had to double back and then they would have been seen," Charlie countered.

Goodwin huffed a little but conceded the point.

"That means our killer is one of three people," Goodwin said and gave a look at the top of the stairs.

"Edward Whitehall, Giorgio Scalfani, or Sylvia Montegard," Charlie said, listing the names.

"Along with Colonel Elmore and Angie Harris, they were the only ones staying on the second and third floors?" Goodwin asked.

Charlie nodded. Three suspects, and Charlie knew, with a bit of dread, who was the most likely.

31

Charlie locked eyes with Goodwin and the Detective frowned.

"I want to speak with Colonel Elmore," Charlie said.

"No," Goodwin replied flatly.

"I think it might help you understand some things," Charlie persisted.

"Like what?" Goodwin asked, a tone of exasperation entering his voice.

"Like who did and who didn't kill Michael Ambrose and Angie Harris, and why," Charlie answered.

"It seems quite obvious to me. Elmore killed Ambrose, and now someone has killed Miss Harris either in a completely unrelated incident, or to cast doubt on the arrest of Colonel Elmore. He may very well have had a conspirator, and if that's the case, we didn't pick them up before for the Ambrose murder, but we will now," Goodwin pronounced and turned to stalk away toward the front door.

"At which point if they were a conspirator, why would they kill Angie? What was there to gain? I mean, you just said it, Detective, by killing Angie they've only exposed themselves as conspirators. They just had to keep quiet and let Elmore rot in a prison cell," Charlie said, stepping along to chase Goodwin down the hall, matching him stride for stride.

Goodwin whirled on him and caused Charlie to falter in his steps to stop quickly.

"Mister Callahan, this is NOT your investigation, and

would appreciate it if you kept your nose out of this. Let me do my job, Charlie, and you concentrate on keeping out of my way. The more you meddle around, the longer it will take!"

"And if you arrest the wrong people for committing these murders, your real murderer will escape and you'll be left trying desperately to chase them down outside of your jurisdiction," Charlie asserted.

Goodwin scowled.

"Fine. Come with me. We'll talk to Elmore together, if his lawyer allows it."

*   *   *

Charlie got out of the blue sedan in front of the police station and followed Detective Goodwin up the concrete stairs into the old brick building. Like much of Falmouth, the police station for Falmouth was a historic building, a quaint brick colonial-style structure that spoke of days gone past when the police might have had horses in the building to the side which now functioned as the police garage and maintenance facility for the handful of cars they had.

Dark stained oak marked offices and separated areas from one another.

Goodwin raised a hand to wave at the desk sergeant who looked up.

"He's with me," Goodwin said and led Charlie through. The desk sergeant went back to reviewing his paperwork, ignoring them as Charlie followed Goodwin past his office and down to the basement stairs. A sign said 'holding cells' with an arrow pointing down the stairwell.

On the way, Goodwin had called an attorney from a firm called Schuster and Brownley, Elmore's defense attorney.

As they walked into the hallway with two cells and one small private room for interrogating prisoners, Elmore's attorney stood from the bench lining one side of the wall, opposite the cells.

"I'm not sure why we're here, Detective, my client has already given you every bit of cooperation and information you've requested, and you've still refused to drop the charges. You know, as we spoke before, that I will be recommending charges for false arrest to my client and a civil suit against the town," Andrew Schuster spoke.

He was a lanky man with salt and pepper hair, and a weak chin. Cornflower blue eyes fixed on Goodwin first, and then switched to Charlie. Schuster looked Charlie up and down and Charlie did the same to get the measure of the man.

Unlike the personal injury attorneys that were all smiles and cheerful attitudes to try to engender some warmth and camaraderie, Andrew Schuster's gray suit and navy blue tie were almost combative. Schuster bristled like a battleship on high alert, ready to blast apart any objection.

"I appreciate your coming down here, and I'm sure that the Colonel will compensate you for a few more questions," Goodwin said, holding a hand up to forestall any further protests.

"Who's your friend?" Schuster asked, nodding at Charlie.

"Charles Callahan. I know Colonel Elmore from his recent past with Michael Ambrose," Charlie said and stretched out a hand. Schuster took it in a firm grip and gave him a quick shake before dropping it.

"And what is your business in the murder charges against my client? Are you a police officer?" Schuster asked pointedly.

"No, I'm apparently a fellow suspect in this whole affair, but I have some information that could lead to exonerating your client. The only way I could talk to him was with Detective Goodwin's permission and with him present, so here we are," Charlie explained.

"A fellow suspect? Then why is MY client in a cell and not this man?" Schuster growled out the question at Detective Goodwin, gesticulating toward Charlie.

"Something I am asking myself more and more," Goodwin grumbled.

Charlie grimaced and cleared his throat.

"There's been a second murder," Charlie explained.

Schuster's face registered shock, then recognition.

"Then, whoever killed this second person is probably the same person who killed Ambrose, which means you have to drop charges immediately against my client and let him out!"

"Not so fast! Your client may have been working with an accomplice, one who was worried about being exposed as Colonel Elmore drew closer to a grand jury indictment, so they killed again. Perhaps Elmore didn't kill anyone, but was merely an accessory," Goodwin pointed out.

"Fine. Let's get this over with then," Schuster said irritably and walked further down the corridor toward the interview room. Charlie followed him as Goodwin got Colonel Elmore out of the holding cell.

"You really think you have evidence that exonerates my client?" Schuster asked once they were alone in the small interview room.

"I think so, if he'll admit to one or two things that are entirely legal. An affair for instance," Charlie hinted.

"What??" Schuster asked. His reaction made it evident

that Elmore was hiding his affair even from his own defense attorney. Charlie's heart sank a bit. He was hoping Schuster would at least know about that. If Elmore's odd personal code of chivalry prevented him from even telling his defense counsel about the affair with Sylvia Montegard, it might be all over. As long as Elmore was sleeping with Sylvia, he wasn't downstairs killing Michael Ambrose. No man could be two places at once.

"It depends on what he admits to, but it could go either way. Actually I'm glad you're here to advise him on which questions to answer and what not to answer," Charlie said with a tone of relief.

Schuster peered at Charlie with a piercing gaze.

"What do you do for a living, Mister Callahan?" the attorney asked.

"I'm a major case adjuster... or I was, for an insurance company here in New England," Charlie answered.

"That explains a lot," Schuster said and visibly relaxed. His gaze remained wary, however, and he looked as though he was about to say something when the door opened and Goodwin led in a tired and bedraggled Colonel David Elmore.

32

David Elmore looked like crap. He was unshaven and looked like he hadn't slept since the day of his arrest. The whole affair had only been two days ago, but he still looked as though he hadn't had any comforts for a week.

"David," Schuster said and walked over to shake his client's hand.

At the sight of his attorney, David transformed from the bedraggled and unkempt man into the officer he was. His back straightened, his gaze cleared, and even somehow his unshaven face seemed a bit more ruggedly handsome and masculine.

"Andrew. Thank God," David said. While his posture spoke to a stiff upper lip attitude, his voice belied his relief. "Mister Callahan? What are you doing here?"

"Colonel, I may have some information that can help get you out of here, but I need your help," Charlie said as he reached out and shook Colonel Elmore's hand.

David Elmore stared at him for a few moments, but nodded cautiously all the same.

"All right, whatever I can do to help, I'll do it," he replied.

"Good. Now Mister Callahan, maybe you can enlighten us all as to the information you alluded to?" Goodwin asked and gestured to the table. Schuster and Elmore sat side by side. Goodwin took a seat and gestured for Charlie to take the seat at his side.

Charlie picked it up and carried it to the long end of the table, sitting on a third side. He didn't feel it particularly appropriate to sit contrary to David or right by his side. He could, after all, be very much incorrect. He'd gone over his self-doubts with his wife.

The trio looked at him expectantly.

"Angie Harris was killed today, perhaps only an hour ago," Charlie said as he folded his hands on the table.

"Angie?? How? What?" David asked, absolutely flummoxed by the news.

"Who is Angie Harris?" Schuster asked.

"Angie Harris is... was, a young journalist who was staying at the B&B where David and I and Michael Ambrose and others were staying," Charlie supplied the answer.

"Why would anyone want to kill her?" Schuster asked.

David nodded earnestly. He wanted to know as well.

"Because she was young, enthusiastic, and had information that would exonerate you," Charlie answered.

"Be specific Mister Callahan, my client is on the line here," the lawyer warned.

"Angie Harris knew that someone else had contact with Michael Ambrose just a short time before he died. She didn't know who it was, but she knew it was not Colonel Elmore. She told me this yesterday," Charlie began.

"And she hid this from me?" Goodwin asked, frowning.

"I don't know why she didn't mention it, but we did speak, and she said that on the night of the murder, she heard Michael and another person talking, a man's voice," Charlie advised. Schuster listened attentively as did David Elmore.

"And that someone heard her confess this and killed her because of that knowledge?" David asked, speaking up. This earned a cautionary touch from his attorney, but the question hung in the air.

"Angie Harris was leading a double life. Has anyone here heard the name Calvin Hodges?" Charlie asked and pulled out his cell phone.

The detective and the colonel shook their heads. Schuster narrowed his gaze ever so slightly.

Charlie opened the phone and brought up the article he'd found earlier that morning. Angie hadn't even had time to request that it be pulled from the papers.

"This article appeared this morning. Yesterday afternoon, Angie and I spoke about my investigation into this whole affair, and this article appeared in this morning's edition. When I confronted Angie about it, she admitted it: Angie Harris was Calvin Hodges. She operated under a pseudonym. She felt that sexism was endemic to the newsroom and the only way to be taken seriously was to publish under a man's name. The killer saw this article too. It details the numerous little inconsistencies that I began to pick apart to create reasonable doubt in this case," Charlie said. Schuster seemed pleased.

"While I would love to release Colonel Elmore, the evidence you're putting forward of this mystery person talking to Ambrose amounts to hearsay. Unless we have it as a dying declaration, or if we had Miss Harris saying it, then it would be different. But we don't," Goodwin pointed out.

"But we don't need it as anything other than support for what Mister Elmore can provide," Charlie said.

Schuster and Goodwin looked at David. Elmore spread his hands with a confused look on his face.

"Where were you on the night that Michael Ambrose died, Colonel Elmore?" Charlie asked directly.

David sighed and shook his head.

"After the argument, I went to sleep in my bed," Elmore

said simply.

"No. You didn't. It was made up by the maids, it had never been slept in, and the bottle of strychnine was tucked under the mattress. A bottle you say you've never seen, and I believe you on that point, Colonel," Charlie said.

Schuster raised a hand.

"That's what the cops say, so what's the point in all this Mister Callahan?"

Goodwin looked at Charlie and frowned.

"I wouldn't mind you getting to the point," the detective said flatly.

"I know where he was the night of the murder. He wasn't in his bed, but he was in A bed: with someone else," Charlie said simply.

David bristled and sat up straighter.

"What are you implying?" Elmore asked with a biting tone.

"I know where you were," Charlie said, "and who you were with."

Elmore's hands clenched in fists.

"What is he talking about, David?" Schuster asked, frowning as he looked to his client and back to Charlie.

"I'm talking about Colonel Elmore having a lover. He has a lover he romanced while Michael Ambrose was speaking with someone else in the living room of the Safe Harbor, a lover he was spending the night with while Michael Ambrose was dying from strychnine poisoning. And that is why he wasn't with Michael Ambrose, wasn't poisoning him, and also wasn't in his own bed, leaving it open for the real killer to slip the bottle between the mattress and boxspring," Charlie said.

Elmore snarled.

"Damnit, you shut up!" he exclaimed and pounded his fists on the table.

"David, if you have an alibi for the murder that rules you out, all you have to do is give the name. Mister Callahan is trying to help you here," Schuster said firmly. "As your attorney, I have to advise you; I think explaining to Detective Goodwin what was actually happening and giving him a name is your best bet. If you cooperate, I can speed things along and we can get you out of here this afternoon," Schuster advised, gripping Elmore's forearm emphatically.

"Colonel Elmore doesn't want to name his lover. It would cause great scandal. But I assure you, if it can be kept quiet, discrete, then I will name her, and if pressed, she will agree and confirm everything I'm saying," Charlie said, looking from Elmore to Schuster and then over Goodwin. The detective looked mystified by this revelation.

"You have an alibi and you decided to conceal it?" Goodwin asked, stabbing the air in an accusatory manner, pointing his finger at Elmore.

"His lover is in a highly precarious position, Detective, one where any scandal leaked to the press by the police department could ruin them," Charlie said, staring at Elmore, meeting his angry gaze. Charlie calmly stared into his eyes and saw the flash of fear, remorse, and concern dance like shadows behind David's angry eyes.

"Sylvia Montegard," Goodwin whispered as it clicked into place.

Elmore growled, but otherwise said nothing.

"Is this true, David?" Schuster asked.

David didn't speak, didn't grunt, didn't move. He simply stared daggers at Charlie.

"She'll confirm it if you can guarantee discretion. I'm

certain even Colonel Elmore will confirm it all if you can keep all of this out of the papers," Charlie said.

"As far as I'm concerned, this is all attorney client privilege. I can't and won't be saying anything to anyone at anytime," Schuster said.

"I'll keep it quiet. I have respect enough for the Colonel and his paramour to take this to my grave. I don't respect foolishness and pride," Charlie said, nodding to the Colonel.

Elmore seemed a bit mollified by this as the three men looked and fixed a gaze on Goodwin.

"I'm not promising anything, but if you confirm who I think it is, or give me a name if it's someone different, I can keep the crime file confidential, and once charges are filed, it will remain sealed," Goodwin said firmly. "It's honestly the best I can do."

Elmore sat, frozen for several moments before he slowly nodded.

"Sylvia and I have maintained a, personal relationship for some time now; and part of our both being here was to meet and continue that relationship," David confessed. "The night Michael Ambrose was killed, I retired early and shut my door, but I went to her bedroom. She has a two story suite that spans the second and third floor. I spent the night with Sylvia Montegard, all night."

Goodwin frowned a bit and Schuster positively beamed.

Before Schuster could ask, Goodwin held up a hand to forestall the question about how quickly they could get Elmore released.

"First thing we have to do is verify your client's story with Mrs. Montegard. Once we do that, we can begin the paperwork, IF his story checks out," Goodwin said and shot a glance at Charlie. "And then we're back to looking for the murderer who has taken not just one, but two lives at this point."

Charlie nodded.

"I have a thought or two on that point as well," Charlie said simply.

"Of course you do, I might have been disappointed if you didn't," Goodwin replied glumly.

Charlie gave Goodwin a small smile as he stood from the table.

"I'll take Mister Callahan back to the B&B and speak with Mrs. Montegard. If she verifies your story, all within the strictest of confidence, I'll order your client to be released. Then we can work on getting to the bottom of this whole thing," Goodwin said to Mister Schuster.

The lawyer nodded sharply and smiled.

"I'll begin the necessary paperwork on our end here at the station, and once you radio in, we can be out of here as quickly as possible," Schuster replied.

Goodwin grunted and left the interview room with

Charlie, shutting and locking the door, giving instructions to the officer outside to take Elmore back to his cell for now and take Schuster to his office in the meantime once they were through conferring.

Charlie walked along with Goodwin to follow him back up the stairs and eventually back to the B&B.

*   *

*

Charlie felt dread forming a knot in the pit of his stomach as the Safe Harbor loomed in the distance and they drove up the driveway. He reflected quietly, with a macabre sense of humor, that the Safe Harbor was anything but for Angie Harris and Michael Ambrose.

"So, are you going to tell me your ideas?" Goodwin asked as he shut the engine off and turned to look at Charlie.

"Let's see if Mrs. Montegard sticks to what she told me and exonerates the Colonel first," Charlie said, hedging his bet a little.

"A little less certain now, are we?" Goodwin asked in almost a mocking tone.

"I always reserve the right to change my mind when confronted by new evidence," Charlie replied and got out of the car. Goodwin did the same and the two walked up the stairs to head in the front door.

Sylvia, Scalfani, and Whitehall were sitting in the kitchen at one of the small tables. Patience was nowhere to be seen.

"I'm going to check on my wife," Charlie said as he walked down the hallway to the back staircase and descended. Goodwin walked into the living room, ready to conduct the interview with Sylvia Montegard.

Charlie walked downstairs and saw the great big gorilla

of an officer standing outside of the room.

"Can I see my wife?" Charlie asked. The officer grunted, but the door opened and Patience's tear-stained face peeked out around the door.

"I'm ok, Charlie," she said softly. Her eyes were bloodshot from her tears. The whole situation of discovering the body of Angie Harris on top of dealing with the stress of the murder of Michael Ambrose was getting to her.

"I love you," he said softly as he peered around the officer who continued to block the door.

"I love you, too," she replied.

Charlie looked up at the officer and frowned.

"Do you think you could step aside even a little bit?" he asked.

The officer rolled his eyes and complied, muttering about disobeying orders.

The moment he was out of the way, Charlie caught Patience up in his arms and held her. A few fresh sobs wracked her tender frame and she buried her face in the crook of his neck, laying her head on his shoulder while his arms enfolded her.

"I want to go home," she said softly. "Please, can we go?"

"Soon, dear, very soon. I've almost got this whole thing wrapped up. Colonel Elmore is going to be released by the end of the day, and I'm going to tell Detective Goodwin everything I know so he can arrest the right person."

She listened and then gave a small sharp nod.

"I love you," Charlie said again, tenderly kissing her forehead.

Patience exhaled a soft sigh of comfort as Charlie patted her back.

"I'll be back, dear," Charlie said quietly and began to

disentangle himself. She gave him one final tight squeeze and backed up, giving him a brave smile.

The officer stepped back in front of the door as Patience closed it, and Charlie headed back up to the main floor.

When Charlie walked into the living room, he met a very upset Sylvia Montegard and a frustrated Goodwin.

"You!" Sylvia snapped loudly and stabbed her finger at Charlie.

Charlie blinked in surprise.

She stalked toward him with purposeful steps.

The crack of her palm against his cheek echoed through the room and sent Charlie's head jerking to the side.

"I'd say that's confirmation enough," Goodwin said with a wry smile crossing his features.

"I trusted you with confidence, Mister Callahan," Sylvia snarled. "I trusted you to keep this a secret and now you've informed the police."

"It was the only way, Mrs. Montegard. With Miss Harris' death, there was no other information that would give David an alibi or get him out of danger," Charlie said with a slight sigh.

Sylvia let out a huff.

"And you swear this will not be leaked to the papers? That this will be entirely confidential?" Sylvia asked, turning to Goodwin with her question.

"It will be sealed and the reasons will be kept from the press. We'll just say we were waiting on verification of an alibi, and when confirmation came in, we released him," Goodwin said with a tone of assurance.

"I'll be contacting my lawyers to keep an eye on this. If there is any breach of confidence, I will have your hide, Detective," Sylvia said with a hiss.

"Is that a threat Mrs. Montegard?" Goodwin asked with a cock of his eyebrow.

"It's a promise, Detective," she replied. Goodwin frowned as Sylvia walked out of the kitchen, to the back staircase, and headed up the stairs to her room.

Charlie and Goodwin stood in the living room alone now.

"Well, now that my best suspect is to be released, do you want to let me in on what you have?" Goodwin asked. "It seems we have two suspects remaining, ruling out you and your wife."

Charlie nodded and pulled his phone from his pocket, opening up the email.

"There's a connection here between Michael Ambrose and one other person. I didn't catch it before and they didn't volunteer the information, either," Charlie explained.

He showed Detective Goodwin the name on the Executor line of the estate.

"And they were upstairs when Angie was killed," Goodwin said, nodding quietly.

"And Angie said it was a male voice she overheard with Michael the night he died. I know that part is inadmissible, but that fact remains regardless of whether or not the court admits it as evidence. Beyond that, we have the bottle of Campari in the trash out back and the fact that his room was right by Elmore's. While David was upstairs on the third floor engaged with Mrs. Montegard, anyone could have stepped into his room and put the vial there without risking being seen or discovered," Charlie explained.

"But Elmore locked his room," Goodwin said.

"No, he didn't. Remember what he told us at the station, Detective? He said he merely shut his door. The room doors in this place don't have automatic locks with key cards. They have deadbolts that lock with a key, a key that David left inside his room, so he left the door unlocked. David wanted his affair to be kept secret. He intended to come down sometime during the middle of the night to enter his room so anyone who might see him get up in the morning would only see him leaving his room, not Mrs. Montegard's," Charlie explained.

Goodwin nodded and let out a heavy sigh.

"So it's either one of these two in the kitchen then," Goodwin said.

"Indeed," Charlie said, "but I don't think it was Scalfani."

34

Goodwin left Charlie in the living room, heading back to the police station to get an arrest warrant and to release Elmore from custody. Charlie sighed a little bit as he walked in front of the large fireplace. He headed over to the piano and stroked his fingers over the keys, tapping a few of the pearly whites, eliciting a string of discordant notes.

"So I heard the Colonel is going to be released," said a voice behind Charlie.

Charlie turned and saw Edward Whitehall standing in the living room with him. He wore a set of jeans and an untucked white oxford style shirt.

"Yes. I found out that he had an alibi," Charlie commented and gave a small smile to Edward. The man smiled back at Charlie.

"Have they got any leads on poor Miss Harris?" Edward asked politely, showing no reaction to Colonel Elmore having an alibi.

"None, really. Just the idea that the two are connected to one another. Whoever killed Ambrose, killed Angie," Charlie answered. He kept his gaze on Edward.

"Mmmm, but suppose Sylvia did it. She drugged Elmore to knock him out and committed the murder," Edward suggested.

Charlie winced to hear his own doubts voiced. He reached the same conclusion before.

"They were lovers, and she went to great lengths to protect him, even asking me to investigate and try to prove his innocence," Charlie replied. "Angie was a help to her. She had information leading to his exoneration, and she even confessed to me that Elmore had an alibi. If Sylvia was the killer, she would have kept the affair a secret, even from me."

"Ah," Edward said with a slow nod as he walked over by the fireplace. His fingers brushed over the mantle as he checked for dust and breathed a heavy sigh.

Charlie withdrew his phone from his pocket and tapped about on the screen, then shoved it back into his pocket.

"Could have been Scalfani," Edward suggested.

"No," Charlie replied, "Scalfani is too moral, too adherent in his faith. You heard him praying at the top of the stairs when Angie was discovered. I confronted him over the reason he was here. He was up to try to get some insider trading information to help his clients recover their money which was heavily invested in Montegard Arms."

"Religion can mask an awful lot of evil," Edward said almost with a laugh.

"It can, but Scalfani also isn't the kind to mix drinks. He lives healthy. It doesn't fit into his character. And when I did confront him about the insider trading, he practically needed to go to confession," Charlie answered. "Religion can mask an awful lot of evil, but it can rub the soul raw with the constant pinprick of a guilty conscience."

Edward gave a small smile and looked down, emitting a tired sigh.

"Seems the list narrows even further, then," Edward said.

"I was out for a walk, then back in my bedroom with my wife by the time the killing occurred," Charlie said as he walked closer to Edward and took up a position at the other edge of the fireplace.

"Hmmm, well, that leaves either the staff, or... me."

"And I think we can agree that the staff had nothing to do with either of these tragic events," Charlie said.

Edward stared at the mantle in silence for a few long moments.

"So, why did you do it? You received quite a hefty share of the settlement. You got to see justice done in the courts," Charlie asked.

"You think money replaces someone like Alli?" Edward asked.

"Nothing can ever replace a life lost, Mister Whitehall. Your sister's death in the trial of the M87 replacement was regrettable, and we all hated that it happened," Charlie said.

"She was more than a sister," Edward said quietly. "She was my twin. My second half. We finished sentences, we saw one another through everything."

Charlie remained silent.

"Money couldn't bring my sister back or replace what was lost. There isn't a price tag on Allison's life. There isn't a way to make it right."

Edward's hand dropped from the mantle.

"So you came to Michael Ambrose late that evening. Offered him a sympathetic ear after the explosive evening. You poured a Campari Spritz, a cocktail of champagne and Campari to mask the bitter taste of the strychnine," Charlie said.

"This is admirable conjecture. But why not ditch the strychnine vial?" Edward asked with a taunting smirk. His hands slipped into his pockets as he stared at Charlie.

"Because it was more important to frame someone else. Particularly Elmore. It was his shoddy paperwork and false record keeping that led to your sister even being in the testing group for a weapons system with known faults to begin with. It wasn't enough to kill Michael Ambrose, the man who directly ordered your sister to take part in the trials. You had to kill two birds with one stone. The vial would implicate Elmore. You got Ambrose drunk. You brought him to his room, then you went back to your own and on the way, you opened Elmore's door. You might even have figured you would plant the evidence later. You saw he wasn't there and slipped in and out ever so quietly."

"Now you're leaping," Edward said, tutting softly with a click of his tongue.

"Except you were overheard. Well after Elmore retired to bed, you were heard up with Michael Ambrose in the living room," Charlie explained.

"And that flimsy excuse is why Angie had to die?" he asked.

"No," Charlie began and looked down at Edward's shoes then back up at him, "no, you were in the kitchen while Angie and I were talking out on the porch. You left your cup in the sink in the kitchen after overhearing the two of us discuss the problems with Elmore's case. Then, the next morning you read the papers as you habitually do. There you saw the article from Calvin Hodges detailing all of the problems with the case, and you realized Angie Harris had a connection, or more likely, was Calvin Hodges. Perhaps you even overheard me warning her right where you're standing. Perhaps you heard her admit to being Calvin Hodges. Such public scrutiny looking into the case would not suit your ends, and you couldn't risk it," Charlie said.

Edward didn't respond, he merely cocked his head to the side.

"You grew desperate. You knew it would only be a

matter of time before Goodwin found out, and Angie was the one who heard you conversing with Ambrose. She was the only one that could place someone else as the last person to see Michael Ambrose alive. You waited patiently for your moment, but you were desperate. Poisoning wouldn't work. So you took the bronze statue from its little display and wrapped it in something, perhaps a pillowcase or a shirt to prevent fingerprinting, and then when you saw her leave to head downstairs, you followed her out and killed her, dropping the statuette and letting it fall behind her down the stairs," Charlie explained.

"This is marvelous for some crime drama or detective show, but you have no proof, Mister Callahan," Edward said.

"I'm certain that a thorough search of your room will yield a bloody pillowcase or shirt or handkerchief, and the fibers will match those found in Angie's scalp. Further, I'm certain that they will find your fingerprints on the Campari bottle. Even if they don't, I'm certain they can trace the purchase with your credit or debit card," Charlie said.

"I have to hand it to you, Mister Callahan, that is a brilliant piece of detective work you've done. But you see, you can't prove it, at all, even that bloody pillowcase, and it was a pillowcase I used, will be useless once it's finished soaking in the bleach in my bathroom sink, and once I kill you, your testimony and deduction will disappear in a puff of smoke, up in flames as it were," Edward said and pointed to the fireplace as he withdrew one hand from his pocket. He wrapped his fingers around the end of the fireplace poker and smiled, raising it up to study the tip. "I'm afraid, Mister Callahan, I can't let you live. You've heard my admission of guilt, and that isn't hearsay. That would be allowed in court."

Edward took a menacing step toward Charlie and he

backed up. Pulling his hand out of his pocket, he held up his phone. A counter with numbers flashing as time passed flickered on his phone screen. A large red recording button saying 'Push To Stop' glowed under the counter.

Charlie gave a small smile. Edward flinched.

"This will be enough," Charlie said and slid it back into his pocket.

"Give that to me!" Edward hissed and stepped forward with another firm step.

Charlie shook his head and stepped back.

Edward lunged at him, bringing the iron poker down in a vicious slash aimed right for Charlie's head.

Charlie ducked off to the side and put a chair between him and the advancing Edward who gripped the side of the chair and toppled it out of his way. Charlie continued to back away, leading Edward on a small chase around the living room, always keeping an eye out. The iron poker swung and narrowly missed Charlie's head once more as he dodged at the last second.

"She was my sister! You don't understand! She was my twin you bastard! And those smug pieces of crap tried to cover it all up, tried to profit off of her death!" Edward shrieked. He brought the poker low this time and swept Charlie's legs from underneath him with a painful crunch.

Charlie fell back as the wind was knocked out of him by the impact.

"I'll kill you and run. The money I got from the settlement will be enough to set me up somewhere else and I'll make sure the press gets ahold of David Elmore screwing Sylvia Montegard behind her husband's back. I'll make sure they get the sordid details of just why Elmore fouled up his paperwork so badly," Edward said and brandished the poker, hot angry tears pouring down his face.

He brought the poker down and the iron tip slammed into the Persian rug with a hefty thud as Charlie rolled to one side.

Edward stepped in and delivered a swift hard kick to Charlie's gut, making him double over in pain.

"You only had to be incompetent. You only had to miss one or two details," Edward said as he reared back once more with the iron poker.

A hand grabbed his forearm and twisted him around. The awful sound of a hard punch smacking into Edward's jaw followed. The poker clattered to the ground as Edward's head snapped to the side with the blow. A follow up punch made Edward groan in pain as the second strike slammed into his gut and a knee came up and crunched into his nose, toppling him backward. Charlie huffed and panted as he tried to catch his breath and scramble to his feet, as David Elmore stood over the limp whining form of Edward Whitehall.

Detective Goodwin stood right behind him.

35

Goodwin got Edward to his feet and Charlie stood up with a hand from Colonel Elmore.

"How are you?" the colonel asked.

"I'm fine, fine," Charlie coughed out the words.

Edward's hands were brought behind his back and he was handcuffed. Goodwin read him his rights and arrested him for assault and attempted murder of one Charles Callahan, and followed it up with the murders of Angie Harris and Michael Ambrose. Edward twisted in the cuffs and tried to wrench free, but to no avail. Once he was in a car on its way to the police station, Goodwin stepped back into the B&B to find Charlie sitting in one of the chairs by the fireplace, a bottled water held in his hands.

"You've been right all along so far, Mister Callahan, as much as it pains me to admit that," Goodwin said. Elmore stood beside Charlie's chair.

"Edward made an admission of guilt to me," Charlie said.

"He told you he did it?" Goodwin asked, marveling.

"He told me he did it, why he did it, and I even got it on tape," Charlie said, pulling his phone out and showing the recording, which he had stopped after his timely rescue. Thankfully, in the scuffle, his phone hadn't been damaged at all.

Goodwin shook his head.

"Amazing! I'm not sure if it's admissible or not, but your testimony will be, combined with all of the other evidence.

have men searching his room right now," Goodwin advised.

"You'll find a pillowcase in his bathroom sink being soaked in bleach. There may be traces of blood left on it. He used the pillowcase to hide prints from the bronze statuette he used to kill Angie. The fibers will match those found in her skull, I'm certain," Charlie said.

"Good to know," Goodwin said.

"The Campari bottle is in situ in the back garbage can. He tossed it there rather than the recycling in his haste. If he'd tossed it in with the rest of the glass and cans, it might never have been found," Charlie said.

"I'll have my people get that as well. I don't say this often, Mister Callahan, but thanks. Your investigation made this case," Goodwin praised.

"And saved me from a lifetime in prison," Elmore added.

"David!" Sylvia's voice echoed out from the back entrance to the living room as she dashed forward and threw herself into his arms.

He caught her in a warm embrace as his arms folded around her, and they kissed in their reunion.

Charlie looked aside and Goodwin coughed, leaving the living room.

Sylvia and David pulled apart from one another. David at least had the good sense to blush, even as Syliva straightened her dress.

"Thank you, Mister Callahan, for saving David," Sylvia said softly.

"Look, I know you may not approve of what's going on between Sylvia and I. But all the same, thank you," Elmore said, guessing at the cause for Charlie's embarrassed silence.

"My approval isn't at issue here. People do a lot of stupid things all the time. I've learned to clean up after people making terrible mistakes. Drinking and driving and other illegal activities go on every single day, and they come across my desk. I don't need to approve. I just need to investigate," Charlie said.

Sylvia seemed mollified by this, as did Colonel Elmore.

"Thank you again for investigating. That investigation without prejudice is what kept me out of prison," David said and reached out to offer a handshake.

Charlie looked at the hand offered and then up to David before he stood and shook his hand.

David smiled. He let go of Charlie's hand and he and Sylvia left Charlie alone in the living room.

Charlie sat once more.

"You have a good man," Charlie heard Sylvia say.

Just as he finished sitting, Charlie stood up. Patience dashed forward and he caught her in his arms, holding his wife close.

She kissed his cheeks and his forehead and he kissed her cheeks and her jaw.

"Are you ok? They told me that Mister Whitehall attacked you!" she exclaimed.

"I'm fine... really, I am, sweetheart. The colonel intervened just in time and saved me from a fateful encounter with an iron poker," Charlie said with a smile as he held the love of his life in his embrace. He looked into her eyes with his own and she stared lovingly back into his gaze.

"From now on, I plan our anniversary getaways," she said with a nervous laugh.

Charlie chuckled lightly, then let loose into a roaring laugh.

Charlie shut the trunk as the last of their bags were put inside. He got in with Patience, and they left the Safe Harbor B&B behind. It was Monday after the long weekend, and Charlie drove through the sleepy town of Falmouth as he headed for the interstate to take them over the bridge and back to the rest of Massachusetts and, from there, on to Connecticut.

"But seriously, next year, you owe me big, buster. Hawaii at least," Patience teased him. Her hand reached out for his and Charlie squeezed her hand tenderly, driving with the other hand.

"Would you settle for Hartford? Or maybe Harrisburg, PA?" he asked teasingly.

"Nothing less than Maui," she stated imperiously with a little sniff from her nose. "Honestly, Charles Francis Callahan, two murders is NOT the way to celebrate our anniversary."

"No one can say it wasn't a lively weekend, though!" he joked.

She groaned.

"Sorry," he apologized.

Before she could respond, the dashboard console lit up with an incoming call from Charlie's phone.

'WORK' flashed across the screen with a green phone to accept and a red phone to refuse displayed underneath.

Charlie removed his hand from hers and hit the 'Accept' button on the steering wheel.

"This is Charlie," he said by way of a greeting.

"Callahan?" came a male's voice. Charlie's boss, Darren, was on the line.

"Yeah, it's me. What can I do for you Darren?" Charlie asked.

"I'm sitting in my office with Heather from HR and our VP, Angela. Some things have come across my desk, Charlie, that we just can't ignore," Darren said.

Charlie felt his stomach sink. Patience's smile vanished, her lips forming into a thin line of concern.

"IT reports that you used Hawthorne's login on your work laptop while you were suspended and accessed a file? You DO know that you were suspended and you were NOT supposed to be accessing work materials, right? That's why we locked your account over the weekend. We got a ping that you had logged in and, maybe this was my fault, Charlie, but I thought it was crystal clear that you were on suspension for making such a cock-up of the Montegard claim," Darren said.

Charlie was silent.

"Mister Callahan, are you there?" Angela's voice cut in.

"Yes, I'm here," Charlie said.

"Mister Callahan, when you were suspended, your boss was supposed to revoke your claim system and remote access while we reviewed your work and your employment with us to determine if we were going to continue our relationship with you as our employee," the HR manager said. "We'd like an explanation as to why you used another team member's login on your company issued laptop to access a program your own access was cut off for while you were on suspension. This is VERY serious, Mister Callahan, I hope you understand what we're talking about here."

"I do," Charlie replied.

"Well, Charlie? Do you have an explanation? Tell me what happened. Why were you online and accessing the platform while you were on suspension?" Darren pressed, a note of desperation in his voice.

"I'm sure you saw the newspapers? The murders in Falmouth?" Charlie asked.

There was a moment or two of silence as they spoke.

"I have, Mister Callahan, but what does that have to do with your accessing systems you were not supposed to access?" Angela asked pointedly.

"I was investigating the murders. They centered around the Montegard claim. There was pertinent information that-" Charlie began.

"So you accessed private information? We received no court order or subpoena for our claim file information, no request from Falmouth police. You took it on yourself to access private information and hand it over while you were on suspension? Is that it?" Angela asked, accusingly.

Charlie grew silent again.

"Is she right, Charlie? Is that what happened?" Darren asked.

"Yes. They originally arrested the wrong man for the murders. The claim file was a big help in identifying who did it, and I was asked to investigate this-" Charlie began again.

"So you were asked to investigate this incident and chose to breach corporate policy about claims platform access and forcibly take information by logging in under one of your coworkers' logins? You took on a matter that was a conflict of interest, requiring you to breach our corporate privacy policies, and didn't bother to even contact your supervisor, all while you were on suspension?" Angela cut in once more.

Charlie sighed.

"Is that accurate Mister Callahan?" The HR manager asked once more.

"Yes," Charlie answered simply. Patience reached over and gave his hand a squeeze.

There were a few moments of silence over the phone.

"I hate having to do this over the phone, Mister Callahan, but effective immediately, you are no longer an employee of Allied Assurance General Insurance Companies or any of its subsidiaries. Tomorrow, a representative of the company will be at your house to pick up your laptop and any other company issued equipment, and you will not be eligible for rehire," Angela said firmly, a note of bitterness in her voice.

Charlie was silent and the pit of his stomach dropping turned into a twisted knot.

"Are you there, Mister Callahan?" Heather's softer voice came over the phone.

"Yes," Charlie replied.

"Do you understand, Charlie?" Darren asked.

"I understand. I'm fired. I'm done. I no longer work for you and someone is going to come by and grab my laptop and backpack and mouse tomorrow," Charlie said somberly.

"I might have been able to make a case to keep you on Charlie, but after this, my hands are tied," Darren said with a heavy sigh.

"I get it. Look, I'm in the car on my way home from my anniversary trip with my wife, so do you think I can hang up and call this done now?" Charlie asked.

"Oh! Mister Callahan, I'm so sorry. We didn't know that this wasn't a good time," Heather said.

"Yeah, well, see someone tomorrow. Bye," Charlie said and his thumb pushed the 'hang up' button on the steering wheel.

Charlie sighed heavily as the phone beeped and ended the call.

"As if there's ever a good time to call someone and tell them they're fired after they just solved a murder mystery that had the local police completely lost," Patience muttered.

Charlie drove in silence.

"We'll make it work," she said softly.

Charlie grunted his agreement.

She reached over and took his hand in his. Charlie sighed and squeezed her hand in return. As they passed a sign that said 'Scenic Overlook', he pulled over to a small turnoff along the interstate and parked the car. He let go of Patience's hand and stepped out.

She quickly unbuckled her seatbelt and followed, not quite sure if her husband was about to pitch himself over that 'scenic overlook' or not. Charlie just leaned against the railing and looked out over the rocks that tumbled away below toward the sea.

"Honey?" she asked.

"In a way, I'm relieved. Yanno? It's stressful, of course, but now I don't have it hanging over my head any more," Charlie said.

"Yeah?" she asked and embraced his arm as she stood beside him.

"Yeah. I mean, now I'm free to pursue whatever other job I can get as a recently fired insurance adjuster who violated corporate ethics," he said.

"Ohhhh," Patience moaned a little bit and gave his arm another comforting squeeze.

Charlie turned and favored her with a tired, genuine smile.

"I got you. I have my faith. I have my health. I have my family. What more do I need?" Charlie asked softly. He leaned over and kissed Patience tenderly on the forehead.

"I'm glad to hear you say that," she said, leaning into the kiss.

"Just gotta figure out how to provide for us is all, how to make sure I can bring some money into the household," he said with a slight nod.

"You did a good job as a detective," Patience said with a smile, only half joking.

Charlie nodded a bit, thoughtfully.

"You think I could?" he asked her curiously.

She realized that he was serious.

"I do. I mean it would take some doing, but we're in a good spot financially. We have savings we can borrow on, and if you put your heart into it, you just proved you have what it takes to be a private detective," she said firmly, with the faith only a dedicated spouse could have.

"It'll mean a lot of late nights, a lot of weekends, and probably a lot of frustration," Charlie said.

"We'll manage," she replied.

"Good thing I'm not short on Patience," Charlie joked and gave her a wink.

She groaned.

"Maybe I should shove you off this cliff right now and save myself the trouble of these bad jokes," she grumbled.

He laughed.

She broke into a smile.

Charlie gave her a kiss on her cheek and the two got back into the car to head home.